STORIES FROM A SMALL TOWN
with a Generous Scoop of Good Will

Coleman Springs USA

GLENN DROMGOOLE

Abilene Christian University Press

COLEMAN SPRINGS, USA

Stories from a small town with a generous scoop of good will

ACU
PRESS

Copyright 2012 by Glenn Dromgoole

ISBN 978-0-89112-319-4

Printed in the United States of America

Coleman Springs, USA is a work of fiction. Some characters may be loosely based on real-life people the author has known or heard about. Others are totally made up.

Cover design by Greg Golden
Interior text design by Sandy Armstrong

For information contact:
Abilene Christian University Press
1626 Campus Court
Abilene, Texas 79601

1-877-816-4455 toll free
www.abilenechristianuniversitypress.com

12 13 14 15 16 17 / 7 6 5 4 3 2 1

Contents

Introduction

The Postmaster

My name is A. M. Spearman, and I'm the postmaster at Coleman Springs, a little town you've probably never heard of.

Everyone calls me Mac, which is short for McDonald, my middle name. I've been the postmaster at Coleman Springs for more than thirty-five years, and while I may not be the oldest postmaster in the country, I'm probably in the top ten. Most people retire when they hit sixty-five, but not me. I enjoy what I do, and mostly I enjoy the people who come by the post office every day.

Nearly everyone in Coleman Springs comes in every day to check their mailbox. Besides the mail, they come to visit, pass the time, gossip, and catch up on what's going on. We don't have a local newspaper anymore in Coleman Springs. We used to—the *Coleman Springs Leader*—but it closed quite a few years ago when the editor got too old and no one else wanted to take it over. Coleman Springs, after all, only has about eight hundred people now. It was bigger

7

back in the fifties and early sixties—we had more than 1,100 residents in the 1960 census—but like many small towns it has gradually lost population as young people have grown up and moved away to the bigger cities where the better jobs are.

Coleman Springs is probably like a lot of little towns you pass through—that is, if you get off the interstate highway. We're not on the interstate, which is another reason we've lost population. We're at the intersection of two state highways and so we get quite a bit of traffic through here, but nothing like an interstate.

But let's say you've passed through a town like Coleman Springs and you've thought, "I wonder what kind of people live here. I wonder what life is like in this little town." Well, that's what I am going to try to tell you.

I'm not saying Coleman Springs is a typical small town. We feel we are several rungs up the ladder from typical. Every town has its own history, its own characters, its own peculiarities, its own issues, and no two towns are exactly alike; and maybe every town feels there is no place quite like it. They're probably right. Certainly we feel that way in Coleman Springs.

If you're looking for sex and scandal, you're in the wrong place. I might get a little personal now and then, but I'm not going to hang people's dirty linen out to dry. We don't do that, or at least I don't do that.

I think you will enjoy meeting the people here. Like any town, I suppose, we have some folks who are a bit hard to take, but all in all the good ones more than compensate for the others.

Coleman Springs has never been a big town, although it's been bigger than it is now. The reason we've survived as well as we have is because we are only thirty-two miles away from the nearest big city, Granger Falls, population about 85,000. People move out here so they can build a house on an acre of land and send their children to a small-town school with a good reputation and not pay the high city taxes. We're not growing, but we've quit shrinking. We are holding our own, which is better than a lot of towns our size.

The big event in our history was the train robbery in 1897. A nine-man gang of armed, masked men held up the train as it slowed down about a mile out of town. They got away with the payroll for the F&S Railroad and also unburdened the women passengers of their jewels and handbags and the men of their watches and wallets.

Four of the bandits escaped, but the other five were caught and killed in a shootout about five miles out of town by a posse organized by Deputy Sheriff Bryant, my wife's grandfather. The F&S never was robbed again, but the payroll and the jewels and watches weren't recovered either. Some say they are buried outside of town, but I think that's just a myth.

Sometime in the 1920s Coleman Springs High School adopted the name "Bandits" as the school mascot, and that's what it has remained until this day. When girls started playing sports, they became the Lady Bandits. A few years ago the state erected a historical marker at the site of the train robbery.

Our town has a grocery and drug store, a dollar store, a hardware store, a bank, a doctor's clinic, a law office, a real estate office, a feed store, an insurance office, three places to eat, a barber shop two beauty shops, two convenience stores with gas pumps, and two taverns or beer joints. We have five churches—Baptist, Methodist, Presbyterian, Catholic, and one non-denominational. The churches outnumber the saloons five to two, which most people in town feel is a good thing.

We are not the county seat, but we do have what in most county-seat towns would be regarded as a courthouse square. Except, instead of a courthouse, we have the post office. It sits squarely in the middle of the square, where the courthouse normally would be, and has two large picture windows, which is another reason I am able to observe and record nearly everything that goes on in town.

Welcome to Coleman Springs.

1

Ida Mae's Adventure

Louise Happenhouser is picking up the mail this week for her sister and brother-in-law while they're in Hawaii.

Louise—or Lou as she's known to everyone in Coleman Springs—has been virtually all over the world herself. She's outlived two husbands and out-lawyered two more and her daddy left her well off in the first place. So she can pretty much go where she wants to when she wants to.

But this week she's happy to be staying at home looking after Howard and Ida Mae Gentry's house and affairs while they are gone to Hawaii.

Lou never thought she would see the day when Ida Mae would get on an airplane to go anywhere, much less all the way to Honolulu. It wasn't that Ida Mae and Howard couldn't afford to travel. Ida Mae had the same daddy as Lou, and he left her just as well off, and Howard made a good living in the insurance business before retiring several years ago.

They've had plenty of time to travel since Howard retired, so that hasn't been their excuse for not going anywhere. No, it goes deeper than that. At least that's what Lou says.

Ida Mae herself was an English teacher years ago, before it just got too hard what with all the kids growing up listening to bad grammar on TV. She bit her lip so hard it would bleed when hearing good students, students who ought to know better, and even fellow faculty members, say things like, "Do you want to go to the game with James and I on Friday night?" And then when even the A and B students, not just the C and D students, started coming in saying, "Me and John had a great time last weekend," Ida Mae just couldn't take it anymore.

She quit teaching and retreated to the grammatical sanctity of her home and tended her flowers and read good books and alphabetized the clothes in her closet—blouses (beige, black, blue, gray, green, orange, red, white, yellow); dresses (beige, black, blue, etc.); skirts (beige, black, blue, etc.)—and listened to public radio, venturing out only on occasion to insist on Howard taking them to the city for a symphony concert.

Well, of course, she had to go out every Wednesday to have her hair fixed and then to the grocery store, but she would go early in the morning at a time when she would be less likely to encounter people who might utter slang or a double negative.

And, Lou says, that's why Ida Mae and Howard never traveled anywhere except by car. Ida Mae wasn't afraid of the airplane crashing. No, she worried that she would be settled into her seat, the latest copy of *The New Yorker* in her lap, when the captain would come on the PA system and announce, "Folks, me and the rest of the crew want to thank you for flying with us today, and if we can do anything to make your flight more pleasant, please let the flight attendants or I know."

Ida Mae was afraid that she would bolt from her seat and attack the pilot's cabin, screaming, "If you cannot speak properly, how can you possibly fly this airplane safely?" She would have to be physically restrained while she continued to rant, "If you do not understand the use of subjective and objective pronouns, you are not qualified to be the pilot and make public announcements over the loud speaker. How dare you insult my intelligence and assault my ears with such appalling grammar?"

That's why Ida Mae and Howard never went anywhere, according to Lou, until this week.

For years Howard had wanted to fly to Hawaii to visit his brother Arthur there. Arthur and Mamie had been to Coleman Springs on several occasions, but Howard and Ida Mae had never been to Honolulu to see them.

Howard had pleaded with Ida Mae to just try it. "Most pilots are well-educated," he suggested. "And surely they have been trained to speak properly when addressing passengers on the microphone."

But Ida Mae couldn't take that chance. Howard didn't want to go without her, so they stayed home.

Then one day Howard was at Coleman Springs Hardware and saw this music contraption that Morris Jenkins was selling. Howard had seen some of the kids wearing them around town but really didn't understand what they were.

Morris showed him how you can load music from CDs onto the machine or download songs from the Internet and then put an earplug in your ear and listen to all your favorite music with no interruptions.

"It just slips in your ear like that?" Howard said. "It doesn't even mess up your hair?"

Howard asked Morris if he would fill the machine with music for him. Morris said he could get one of the high school kids who worked for him to do it. "The kids are a lot better and a lot faster than I am," he said.

Howard went home and collected symphonic recordings, chamber music, piano concertos—dozens of CDs—and took them to the hardware store. The kids had no idea what kind of music it was, but they recorded it into the machine and showed Howard how to work it.

Three weeks ago he presented it to Ida Mae. Of course, she was skeptical at first. Ida Mae doesn't even have a cell phone or a computer, and she wasn't sure about plugging this contraption into her ear.

But once she tried it, she fell in love with it. She would listen to it while working in her garden, while reading her books, while driving to the grocery store, even while getting her hair fixed.

After about a week, Howard dropped the other shoe.

"Ida Mae," he said, "we're going to Hawaii."

"What?" Ida Mae said. "Wait a minute, let me take this plug out of my ear."

"Ida Mae," he said, "we're going to Hawaii. You can take your music box and listen to it all the way there and you won't be able to hear anything anyone says, including the pilot."

Howard had her there, she knew. Ida Mae didn't even put up a fight. She went to her closet and started going through the alphabetized blouses and dresses and skirts and packed for the trip.

2

Banjo's Beard

I certainly didn't recognize Banjo Matson when he stopped by the post office this afternoon.

For as long as anyone can remember, Banjo has sported a long white beard. Almost like Santa Claus except for the fact that Banjo is small and thin. The beard was, at one time, a little more blondish but never dark. In recent years it has been snow white, like the hair on the top of his head.

Well, today there was no beard. Banjo was clean-shaven. Not even a moustache. I really didn't know who he was until he said, "Mac, it's me, Banjo."

It sure sounded like Banjo all right. But this no-beard thing is going to take a little getting used to.

Of course, I asked what everyone else was asking, "What happened to your beard?"

"Well, Mac, you know my little grandson was visiting last week," Banjo said. The boy is five or six and lives in another state. This was the first time he had come by himself

16

to visit Grandpa Joe, as he calls Banjo. Banjo took him around all over town showing him off. A prouder Grandpa I've never seen.

"Anyway," Banjo went on, "the last night he was here, he said, 'Grandpa Joe?' I said, 'Yes.' He said, 'Do you sleep with your beard on top of the cover or under the cover?'

"I said, 'Son, I guess I've never thought about it. I'll check tonight and let you know in the morning.'

"That night after he was asleep, I was about to drift off myself when I started thinking about his question.

"I put the beard under the cover. That didn't feel right.

"I put it on top of the cover. That didn't feel right.

"For more than an hour I kept putting it under the cover, then on top of the cover. It didn't seem right either way.

"Finally, Mac, I just got up and shaved it off!"

Several folks who were listening to the story started laughing. Banjo gave me a little wink.

I'm pretty sure that's the same story I heard my father tell about *his* grandfather back when I was a kid.

After everyone left except Banjo, I said, "All right, Banjo, now what's the real story?"

He looked at me and smiled. "Well, Mac, I have a little growth on my throat, and they're going to put me in the hospital and operate on it. I don't think it's anything serious, but the doctor said I would have to shave off the beard.

"I just thought it would be more fun to tell it the other way.

"I did shave it off while the boy was here, though, so he would be the first to see me without the beard. He thought it was pretty funny, and I gave him a piece of it in a plastic baggie to take home."

"That's a pretty original Coleman Springs souvenir all right," I said.

3

He Could Fix Anything

"He could fix anything."

That's what they inscribed on Possum Johnson's tombstone.

Possum knew he was going to die for several weeks, and he had made his peace with the world. He also told his brother, Otis, what he wanted his tombstone to say. "Might as well say, 'He could fix anything.' That's what they'll all remember me for."

And that was true. It didn't matter if your washer or dryer had quit working, or your TV or air-conditioner had gone out, or something was wrong with your car or motorcycle or boat, Possum could fix it. I don't mean he would *try* to fix it. I mean he would fix it.

Oh, occasionally there would be something that would be beyond repair, but you usually knew that before Possum had to tell you. In that case, you would just tell him to get rid of it for you—but, of course, he didn't. He just tossed it somewhere in the back of his workshop, or in the back yard, and kept it for spare parts. Didn't matter if it was a refrigerator or a radio or a computer. Eventually, he found some use for at least part of the machine.

Now computers were kind of a challenge for Possum at first. But it wasn't too long before he got the hang of them. A computer, after all, is just a machine, and there wasn't a machine alive that could outsmart Possum Johnson for very long. He fixed many a cell phone and fax machine, too.

We're really going to miss Possum around here. There aren't many people in a town who are actually irreplaceable, as much as we might like to think we are. But Possum—well, I doubt we'll ever find anyone like him again.

You're probably wondering how Possum got his nickname, and I'm afraid I don't know. He's been Possum for as long as I've known him, and I guess I've known him pretty much all his life. They started calling him Possum when he was a toddler, and it just stuck with him.

The obituary notice in the city paper listed him as Possum Johnson. At his funeral Elliott Sanders, the pastor of The Church of the Living Word, called him Possum. He said when Possum was ordained as an elder in the church, he asked to be ordained as Brother Possum. "It sounded like something from a children's story," the pastor said, and everyone laughed.

Brother Possum's primary responsibility at The Church of the Living Word was, naturally, to fix things. "There's no telling how much money Brother Possum saved us over the years," the preacher said. "And he always did it so willingly, so cheerfully. I told him one time that his ability to fix things was truly a gift from God, and he laughed and said, 'Oh, preacher, anyone can do what I do.' And I told him, 'That's how you know it is a gift from God, when something comes so naturally to you.' He thought about that a minute and said, 'Well, I'll be danged.'"

The funeral procession from the church to Rosemont Cemetery stretched for at least half a mile. Ironically, two cars overheated along the way and had to be parked on the side of the road.

Possum Johnson would have had them running in no time.

Possum Johnson. "He could fix anything."

4

Daniel Boone and Marshal Dillon

People in Coleman Springs like to take visitors over to meet Daniel Boone and Marshal Dillon.

Sometimes folks run into them in the post office because Daniel and Marshal come in every day to get their mail.

But you are more likely to find them at Daniel Boone & Marshal Dillon Express, our eighteen-hour convenience store a couple of blocks off the square on the state highway. Daniel Boone & Marshal Dillon Express is open from 5 AM to 11 PM seven days a week. Daniel and Marshal operate it.

It's rare that you find them both there at the same time. Daniel, an early riser, works from 5 AM to 2 PM. Marshal, who prefers to sleep late, comes in at 2 PM and closes the store around 11.

Oh, yes, I didn't mention that Daniel Boone and Marshal Dillon are brothers. And, when you look at them, you realize something else. These dark-skinned guys from India have a sense of humor.

They weren't born Daniel Boone and Marshal Dillon. They weren't born in the US. They came over here from India through family connections, and after working in various family enterprises they acquired enough money to buy their own store.

The brothers changed their names, legally, to Daniel Boone and Marshal Dillon. Then they bought the E-Z Time convenience store in Coleman Springs, which was so cluttered and filthy that people stopped there only as a last resort. Gasoline was a nickel a gallon higher, the coffee was bitter, the donuts were stale, the bathrooms were dirty.

Daniel and Marshal fixed all that, almost overnight. First, they closed the store for two weeks and put in new fixtures and new décor and reduced the clutter. They remodeled and upgraded the bathrooms. When they reopened, they dropped gasoline prices to three cents below their competitors, brewed fresh coffee throughout the day, and kept the donuts fresh and the bathrooms sanitized. They put up statues on either side of the front door of the real Daniel Boone and the TV Marshal Dillon. They greeted customers when they walked in the door with a friendly "Howdy!"

People in Coleman Springs don't warm up very quickly to strangers, especially strangers who are obviously from Somewhere Else. So I was surprised at how quickly Daniel and Marshal were accepted.

I don't know if it was their smiles or their business acumen that won people over. Maybe it was the clean restrooms. Whatever the reason, when visitors come to Coleman Springs, we make it a point to take them to meet Daniel Boone and Marshal Dillon and get their authentic autographs.

5

The Good Doctor

My good friend Dr. Taylor Campbell grew up in Coleman Springs, then came back to practice here after medical school.

He is the third Doctor Campbell we've had in Coleman Springs. His uncle was Dr. Theo Campbell, and Taylor took over Theo's clinic when he came home. Theo moved to Virginia to teach in a medical school.

Our first Doctor Campbell was Taylor's grandfather, Dr. Columbus Campbell. Columbus grew up on a farm outside of town, and he figured he would be a farmer like his father and his grandfather. He loved the farm, and he didn't mind the hard work required. He would get up early and milk the cows before going to school, and on weekends he could be counted on to hitch up the mules and plow the fields from sunup to sundown.

Columbus was very bright, and his mother decided early on that he had a future outside of farming. She saved the money she made from selling eggs and that helped send

him through college and on to medical school. Columbus, of course, worked. He waited tables, shoed horses, cleaned buildings, whatever it took to earn his room and board and cover the rest of his tuition.

Dr. Columbus Campbell was the first full-time, sober doctor that Coleman Springs ever had. There had been a couple of so-called doctors who came to town in their wagons once or twice a month with their patented medicines and cure-alls. And there was old Dr. Jonas, but he was drunk most of the time he was here, which wasn't but a couple of years.

Dr. Campbell established the clinic that his son, Theo, eventually took over, and his grandson, Taylor, still operates. He was a good doctor, and he treated everyone in town with respect, regardless of their social or economic standing. He also made house calls when he needed to, and Taylor still does when the occasion demands it.

At one point early in his practice, Columbus took a stand against the Ku Klux Klan, back in its heyday. The Klan held a narrowly defined view of what constituted acceptable lineage and behavior, and Dr. Campbell pretty much ignored their prejudiced proclamations. He openly opposed the candidate the Klan was supporting for mayor of Coleman Springs.

Late one night, the Klan paid a visit to his home. They gathered en masse on his front lawn. Dr. Campbell opened his front door, walked out to the hooded men, and asked the nature of their business.

The leader declared that if he continued to ignore the Klan or oppose its candidate, they would see to it that his clinic was either shut down or burned down.

Dr. Campbell put his hands in his pockets and looked at first one and then the other until his gaze had penetrated each man present.

Finally, he spoke, very calmly. "You think I don't know who you are behind your masks? I could call each one of you by name, and recite your height, weight, and heart rate, and those of your wives and children. I will not succumb to your campaign of fear and prejudice. You do not scare me."

He paused, remaining calm, his hands still in his pockets.

"I have treated every one of you, and all of your families. If you want to shut down or burn down my clinic, you just go right ahead. If you think Coleman Springs doesn't need a doctor and a clinic, well, gentlemen, I have not forgotten how to plow."

With that he turned and walked back into his house.

One by one, the robed and masked men walked away. Columbus Campbell never heard from them again, nor did anyone else in Coleman Springs. Their candidate lost in a landslide.

6

There Am I

It rained so hard last night that even the Baptists didn't show up for Sunday night church. Well, a few did.

Four, not counting the preacher and his wife.

The Rev. Andrew Baker was telling me about it this morning when he came in to mail a package to his brother, who is an Army chaplain in Germany.

"You know, Mac, Baptists usually aren't afraid of a little water. We've all been held under for a few seconds anyway," Brother Andy said. "Now Methodists and Presbyterians might be a little shy when there's a downpour, but not Baptists. But last night even Baptists were afraid to get out."

"So," I asked, "did you cancel services since only a few people showed up?"

"No," he said. "I went ahead and preached."

"But to just four people, not counting your wife?"

"Let me tell you a little story, Mac," he said. "When I was a young preacher just starting out, I was invited to preach

at a little country church on a Sunday night. I didn't get a chance to preach very often—I was just starting seminary—so I was excited about it.

"But that Sunday night was kind of like last night. The bottom dropped out. It thundered and lightninged and poured, and when we got ready to have church, only three people were there, plus Mrs. Vernon (the woman who had invited me to preach) and me.

"She apologized for the small turnout, and I said that no one could predict anything like this. I just assumed we wouldn't have church that night. I told her that I appreciated her inviting me, but I would just have to take—and I actually said this—a rain check.

"She said, 'So you're not going to preach?' And I said, 'Oh, no, not to three or four people. Why don't you just cancel the service considering the circumstances?'"

"She said, 'I'll let you off the hook, but we're going to have church anyway. I'll preach.'

"I said, 'I've never heard a woman preach. I think I'll stick around.'

"And that's what I did. We sang a couple of hymns, even though the pianist hadn't weathered the storm, so we sang a cappella, and then Mrs. Vernon got up to preach.

"She said, 'Our scripture tonight is from Matthew 18:20, *Where two or three are gathered together in my name, there am I in the midst of them.*'

"Mac, she wasn't preaching to that little group. She was preaching to me. I've never refused the opportunity to preach since then.

"Last night, when only four people showed up, I preached from that text and told them that story. Actually, it might be one of the best sermons I've ever preached. You should have been there."

I probably should've. But like the other Presbyterians in town, I stayed home, high and dry.

7

Broder and Oder

The Dawkins brothers Broder and Oder, came in together to collect their mail. They had big news. I'm talking *big* news here.

Broder usually comes in by himself, preferring to leave Oder at home. When Oder is with him, no one really wants to visit very long with Broder, and that's really not fair to him. Broder is a nice guy with a heart of gold.

Of course, Oder isn't Oder's real name. His real name is Broderick, which was shortened to Erick, but he became Oder to everyone (except Broder) a long time ago—for what should be obvious reasons.

No one calls Oder that to his face. In fact, when Oder is around, most people don't stick around long enough to call him anything. They just say something like, "Hi, guys!" and wave a big wave and hightail it to somewhere that doesn't smell so bad, like the barnyard or the paper mill.

The problem is that Oder has a condition that makes him smell bad. The condition is that he doesn't ever take a bath.

It's not that Oder—Erick—is retarded or anything. He's not. Well, he's not mentally retarded. He is somewhat socially retarded.

It's just that social amenities such as bathing, brushing one's teeth, applying deodorant to one's underarms, and changing one's underwear aren't all that important to him.

Perhaps he has bigger things on his mind, like saving the planet from global warming. People around here would rather he save this corner of the planet from global stinking.

Well, I told you that Broder and Oder (Erick) had some big news, I mean *big* news.

Here it is: Oder isn't Oder anymore. Oder, I mean Erick, bathed. Brushed his teeth. Deodorized himself. Changed underwear. The whole enchilada.

Broder said one day about two weeks ago Erick woke up, walked outside, took a deep breath of fresh air, strolled over and sniffed the roses growing on the fence, knelt down and smelled the freshly-mowed grass, then came in, took off his clothes, turned on the shower, and spent the next forty-five minutes there. Used almost half a bar of soap. Half a bottle of shampoo.

He stepped out and told Broder, "It smells bad in here. We ought to do something about that."

They threw away Erick's clothes, fumigated the place, called in the carpet cleaners from Granger Falls, and left the windows open for a week. Erick bathed twice a day, sometimes three times.

Broder just sat there astonished. Relieved, of course, but in shock. What had happened to Oder? Why did he decide to become Erick?

Broder doesn't know the answers. He has decided to just accept it as a gift of grace, a gift from God.

And so do we all.

8

The Timms Sisters

I see the four Timms sisters at least two or three times a week. Of course, they aren't Timms anymore, but I still think of them that way.

Patti, Tammi, Cindi, and Ashli all grew up here. Their daddy, Rollie Timms, ran his own highway construction company, which he sold a few years ago for several million dollars. Their mom, Nancy Timms, taught at the high school. Rollie and Nancy are both retired but still live in Coleman Springs. They support every local cause, both with their money and their enthusiasm.

Frankly, I don't know what we would do without the Timms sisters. They've been mainstays at Pioneer Presbyterian Church and have headed up the PTA, the Coleman Springs Garden Club, the Republican Party, the Red Cross, the Women's Bible Study, the Mission Action Project, and the Coleman Springs Book Club. If you need

something accomplished, you get one of the Timms sisters to take charge and it's as good as done.

Their biggest achievement is the Coleman Springs Ice Cream Festival, which they conceived more than a decade ago. It has grown into one of the top festivals in this part of the state and the biggest event we have in Coleman Springs.

The ice cream festival started with a comment from Ashli. She had been to a quilt festival over in Walnut Cove and wondered why we couldn't do something like that in Coleman Springs.

She pitched the idea to her sisters and they jumped at it. But they didn't want to do quilts. After some discussion, they decided that what they really were passionate about was ice cream. So why not an ice cream festival?

"I make the best peach ice cream in the county," said Cindi.

"I'll put up my strawberry ice cream against anybody's," Patti boasted.

"Everybody loves my chocolate chip," Ashli added.

"I can make my pecan praline ice cream," Tammi pitched in. "No one can beat that."

Rollie Timms said he would put a couple of thousand dollars in the pot for advertising the festival. Nancy Timms offered her prize-winning peppermint ice cream as an incentive and said she would get her sister to come to Coleman Springs and serve her very special rum ice cream. You have to experience it—sober—to believe it.

The next thing you knew we had the biggest ice cream festival in the state. Thousands of people come here the second week of July from all over, including dozens of other states, just to hang out and eat ice cream.

Of course, that's not nearly all that the Timms sisters have contributed to our town. Cindi was mayor a few years back—and a very good one at that. She persuaded the four "good old boys" on the town council to make Coleman Springs the second town in the state to pass a citywide no smoking ordinance.

The smoking ordinance was done kind of quietly and some folks didn't like it. In fact, some were downright hostile.

"I'm an Amurican," declared Shorty Hobbes, "and as an Amurican I have an absolute right to smoke, according to the Constitution."

"Show me where in the Constitution it says that," Cindi replied.

And that silenced Shorty because, as Cindi knew, Shorty can't read.

9

Poet Laureate
of Coleman Springs

George Gibbons is the Official Poet Laureate of Coleman Springs. Proclaimed so by the mayor.

George hasn't published any books, although that may change soon. What publisher could resist a book by the Poet Laureate of Coleman Springs after all?

But it really doesn't matter to George. He doesn't write poems to make money. He writes poems to make people happy. He writes poems to make *himself* happy. He writes poems, he told me, because he has to. The poems just come to him as a gift, and he feels obligated to share them.

And share them he does. During National Poetry Month, George decided that it would be great to give everyone in town a poem during the month. So he took a hundred or so of his poems, made three copies of each one, cut them into small pieces of paper and folded them, then put them in a box.

He put a sign on the box: "This is National Poetry Month. Help yourself to a poem. George Gibbons."

He put the box on a little table in front of the post office, and all month long when people came by, they would reach in and pull out a poem. You know, now that I think about it, I don't recall a single person putting it back and taking out a second poem to see if it might be better. Every poem seemed to fit every person.

But that's George. His poems do that. They touch people.

George's poems are very short—three to five lines, occasionally six or eight. He can say more in fewer words than anyone I know. Some of his poems rhyme, some don't. It doesn't matter. What matters is that *they* matter.

All of his poems are signed: G^2.

He composes his poems while driving his delivery truck for Sansom Distributing in Granger Falls. He takes soft drinks around to grocery stores, convenience stores, restaurants, and other businesses all over this area.

He has time to think while he's driving, and he also comes up with ideas, he told me, from the people he deals with.

Let's say, for example, that one of his customers always greets him with a smile. That's a poem. Another one always has a story to tell. That's a poem. Another one is sad. He is inspired to write a poem to cheer her up. Another one always seems mad. He wants to write a poem to help him see the brighter side.

I cherish the poems he has brought me over the years. This one is my favorite.

They come in here
With a purpose
But they leave here
With a smile.

I have that one posted where I can see it every day. It's as if George wrote it for me as a pledge, or a mission statement. It reminds me that that is what I should strive for, with every person who comes in the door. It says more about customer service than whole textbooks on the subject. I sent a copy to the Postmaster General and suggested it be posted at every window at every post office in the country. Unfortunately, it wasn't.

George has probably given that same poem to several other folks, but it doesn't matter. To me, it is the special poem he wrote—in his own handwriting—just for me.

That's why his box during National Poetry Month was so popular. Everyone felt the same way I did.

Mayor Drexel Bryant, for instance, came by and reached in and pulled out this plum:

Be of good cheer—
Your giving
Of your time
Makes life
Worth living
Around here.

Now anyone could have pulled out that poem from the box, and in fact two other people did because George made three copies of each poem. But to the mayor, it was like, "Yes! That's what I'm trying to do."

So Mayor Bryant and the city council unanimously voted to confer upon George the title of Poet Laureate of Coleman Springs. Gave him a framed certificate, signed by all of them.

I would have signed it, too, if they had asked. So would everyone else in town.

Thanks George.

10

The Singing Barber

Pierce Brock is a big man with a booming voice. He was big back in high school when he was an all-district tackle for the Coleman Springs Bandits. And he is quite a bit bigger today, to put it charitably.

Pierce operates the Coleman Springs Barber Shop on the square. The shop has two chairs but just one barber—Pierce. At one time years ago when Old Man Heffington ran the shop, there were two barbers. Old Man Heffington always kept another barber around, mainly because a lot of men refused to let the Old Man cut their hair anymore. He was, after all, legally blind.

The last barber to go to work for the Old Man was Pierce Brock. Pierce went to barber school after high school, then spent several years in the Air Force and barbered in a couple of other towns before coming home. He took second chair at the shop, but only for about six months. Old Man Heffington got to where even he realized he needed to retire, so he sold the shop to Pierce and moved to Florida to live near his son.

Pierce never even thought of hiring another barber. There isn't that much demand for barbers in Coleman Springs, and Pierce figured he could handle the work load just fine.

And now he could sing.

Besides football, the other thing that Pierce Brock loved in high school was singing. He sang baritone/bass with the high school choir and was its most popular soloist. He also had the lead in the Junior-Senior Class Musical—even though he was only a sophomore. He sang at church as well.

Even as a teenager, Pierce was not the least bit shy when it came to singing. He would be out with friends, just driving around, and Pierce would start singing. His friends kidded him about it, but they also realized he was quite good.

During his senior year, however, Pierce changed. His parents had some trouble that I don't want to go into, and Pierce had to go to work to help support the family. Barber school seemed an expedient route to a career, so Pierce worked nights and went to barber school during the day and got his license.

Pierce never really lost his love for music, and in the Air Force he sang with a men's quartet that developed quite a following on base. Now that he owned his own barber shop, he could sing when he felt like it.

Pierce likes the Broadway show tunes, Americana folk favorites, and old gospel hymns, and as word began to spread, men started driving over from other towns to have their hair cut by the singing barber.

He also makes up some of his own songs, one of which has become something of a Coleman Springs Anthem

because he sings it so much in his shop. It's a cheery little
tune that goes like this:

> *I woke up this morning in Coleman Springs,*
> *I woke up this morning in Coleman Springs,*
> *I woke up this morning in Coleman Springs,*
> *And I'm so glad I did.*
>
> *I watched the sun rise in Coleman Springs,*
> *I watched the sun rise in Coleman Springs,*
> *I watched the sun rise in Coleman Springs,*
> *And I'm so glad I did.*
>
> *And I'm so glad I did,*
> *And I'm so glad I did,*
> *I woke up this morning in Coleman Springs,*
> *And I'm so glad I did.*
>
> *I met all my friends in Coleman Springs,*
> *I met all my friends in Coleman Springs,*
> *I met all my friends in Coleman Springs,*
> *And I'm so glad I did.*
>
> *I got my hair cut in Coleman Springs,*
> *I got my hair cut in Coleman Springs,*
> *I got my hair cut in Coleman Springs,*
> *And I'm so glad I did.*
>
> *And I'm so glad I did,*
> *And I'm so glad I did,*
> *I woke up this morning in Coleman Springs,*
> *And I'm so glad I did.*

The last verse is a bit commercial, but, hey, it's his own barber shop so I suppose he can be commercial if he wants to.

I've heard folks come in the post office whistling or humming Pierce's little tune. I even do it myself sometimes, usually right after getting my hair cut.

11

Take Me to Your Mayor

It seemed like something from one of those old space alien movies. You know, where the flying saucer drops into the town and these little green men emerge and one of them says in a high-pitched voice, "Take me to your leader."

That's what I thought about this afternoon when seventeen bikers roared up to the parking lot in front of the post office. One of them dismounted and came inside and asked directions to city hall.

He looked like what you might expect the leader of a motorcycle pack or gang or group to look like. Big guy, tattoos on both arms, dressed in black, brown beard with flecks of either gray or lunch.

He spoke in a deep, gruff voice, "We want to see your mayor." He wasn't smiling when he said it.

I told him that city hall was just around the corner. But, I said, if you would like I could call and see if the mayor was in.

"That won't be necessary," he said. And then he walked out and the pack or gang or group or whatever roared off.

I felt I should call my cousin, Mayor Drexel Bryant, and warn him. But he wasn't in. The secretary at city hall, Grace Martin, wasn't sure where he had gone but thought he would be right back.

"You could call him on his cell phone," she said. So I did. No answer. He must have it turned off.

It wasn't long until the motorcycles roared up in front of the post office again. The same big guy came back into the post office.

By now, word had begun to spread about the seventeen motorcycles roaring through town. We might be considered by some to be a sleepy little town, but no one could possibly be sleeping through all that noise.

Folks came out of the bank, out of the hardware store, out of the grocery and drug store, out of the library, out of the barber shop. Including Mayor Drexel Bryant. Drexel had been getting a haircut when all the commotion occurred.

The leader of the pack came in and said, "The mayor wasn't there. Do you know where he might be? You seem like a fella who knows what's going on around here."

"No, I don't know where he is," I began to say, but about that time I saw Drexel walking up to the motorcyclists outside. "Actually, there he is now. He's talking to your friends."

The leader nodded his head and walked out.

I was on duty by myself and couldn't just leave the post office unattended, but I figured no one would be coming in while seventeen motorcycles were parked outside, so I walked out about halfway down the sidewalk to see if I could hear what was going on.

The leader said something to the mayor and then in a loud voice turned to all the people watching from across the street and said, "Why don't you all come over here for a minute?"

Folks seemed a bit wary, of course, but gradually a few brave souls drifted over. I walked to the end of the sidewalk.

Now the leader was addressing the mayor. He looked very serious. "Mister Mayor," he spoke up, "and citizens of Coleman Springs, we are the BBA Bike Club, and we were passing through your town and decided that we all want to move here."

The mayor was, for one of the few times in his life, speechless. The other folks just kind of looked at each other blankly. Uh, we need more people to move to Coleman Springs, we were thinking, but this was not exactly the kind of economic development we quite envisioned for the community.

Then the leader laughed. "I'm just pulling your leg, Mister Mayor," he said, and all the rest of the bikers whooped it up.

"Actually," he went on, "the club wants to present you— as the official leader of Coleman Springs—with a little award that we have."

He reached into the pocket of his motorcycle and pulled out a small plaque.

"Every now and then when we're riding we pick out a town to recognize. Today you're the lucky town."

He held the plaque and read it out loud, "Hear Ye, Hear Ye, On Behalf of the BBA Bike Club, We Do Hereby Declare

That of All the Small Towns in America, This Is Certainly One of Them."

He handed the plaque to an amused, and relieved, Mayor Bryant. Everyone laughed. The leader shook the mayor's hand.

No longer speechless, the mayor smiled and said, "Thank you for this prestigious award. It will hang . . . ." You couldn't hear the rest of what he said because the seventeen members of the BBA Bike Club started their motorcycles, gave a big wave and roared away. They circled the square slowly, making as much racket as they could, waved again, and headed for the highway.

Drexel shook his head in disbelief. "Another day in Coleman Springs!"

12

Mayor Bryant

In a small town like Coleman Springs, you have to be careful what you say about someone, not just because it might get back to them, but also because the person to whom you are speaking may well be related to the person about whom you are speaking.

That's not to say that we practice in-breeding or anything like that. I don't know of anyone who has married their cousin. Well, not their *first* cousin anyway.

Mary and I are good examples. We are both first cousins to the mayor, Drexel Bryant. Nearly everyone knows that, so I rarely have anyone come in to the post office and start griping to me about the mayor.

Drexel is Mary's cousin on his father's side. His father and Mary's father were brothers, who were the sons of our legendary deputy sheriff, Sam Bryant. Drexel is my first cousin on his mother's side. His mother and my father were brother and sister. I'm pretty sure that doesn't make Mary and me related—other than as husband and wife, of course.

Another reason I probably don't hear a lot of complaints about Drexel is that people like him and respect him and are thrilled to have him as our mayor.

Drexel grew up in Coleman Springs, but then he left for college and joined the Navy ROTC and became an officer in the Navy after college. He stayed in the Navy for thirty-three years before retiring as an admiral. He did several tours of duty at the Pentagon and once was a personal aide to the president.

When Drexel—Admiral Bryant—retired, he and Miriam moved back to Coleman Springs. They had had enough of the fast lane and welcomed the chance to slow down a little.

That didn't last long. First, they got involved in the Coleman Springs United Methodist Church. Miriam started teaching a Sunday school class for middle school girls. Drexel, always an early riser, helped form a Methodist Men's Fellowship group that meets for breakfast on Tuesday mornings. He gets there at five o'clock and starts cooking eggs and bacon and biscuits.

Drexel was invited to be on the board of directors at the bank. Miriam joined the Coleman Springs Book Club and soon was elected president. Once a week she helps out with the citywide Mission Action Project.

When Cindi Timms Phillips decided not to run again for mayor, several folks went to Admiral Bryant and pleaded with him to run. Next thing you know, they hadn't been back here even a year and Drexel and Miriam were mayor and first lady of Coleman Springs.

It's not a full-time job. Well, not a *paying* full-time job. Drexel always seems to be on duty, presiding over one thing or another and looking for ways to make the town a little better or sing its praises to the press and the outside world. Miriam didn't grow up around here, but you would never know that from the effusive way she carries on about Coleman Springs. The Bryants have become the town's biggest boosters.

Mary and I call him Drexel, he being our first cousin and all. But most people in town address him as admiral.

Miriam and Drexel came over for dinner the other night. Mary served her famous fried chicken. Admiral Bryant, who has literally lived all over the world, proclaimed it the best chicken on the planet. Miriam agreed and added that not even the White House chef could make a dessert that compared to Mary's banana pudding.

Later in the evening Drexel got to talking about his and Mary's grandfather, Deputy Bryant. He died when Mary was quite young and before Drexel was even born, but they had heard stories all their lives about Sam Bryant, who never learned to drive a car and continued enforcing the law around Coleman Springs on horseback until the day he died.

"He was always one of those larger-than-life figures in my mind," Drexel said. "Even though I never knew him, there were plenty of times during my naval career when I would face a tough situation and I would think, 'What would Deputy Bryant do?' That always seemed to serve me well.

"Once, when we were on the President's staff, I was troubled by a decision the President was about to make. I thought it was wrong, but I hadn't been there very long and wasn't sure I had the right to speak out.

"That night I told Miriam about it . . . ."

Miriam picked up the story. "And I said, 'Drexel, what would Deputy Bryant do?'"

"The next day I told the President how I felt about the issue. I spoke calmly but confidently even though I was the most inexperienced member of his staff.

"There was a long silence. Finally, the President said, 'Admiral, you may be right.' Nothing else was said, but the President took another approach to the problem."

Who could think that the long arm of the law in Coleman Springs would reach all the way to the White House?

"I would like to write a book about Deputy Bryant some day," Drexel said.

"If you can ever find the time," Miriam laughed.

13

Granny B

Mary said to Drexel, "How well do you remember Granny B?"

"Oh, I loved going to Granny B's house," Drexel said. "She had that big old rambling white house and everything in it seemed so old and so proper. And she always had something cooking that smelled good."

Granny B was Mabel Bryant, who was married to Deputy Bryant for forty-two years and outlived him by thirteen years.

"How old were you when she died?" Mary asked.

"I was in fifth grade, so I must have been ten or eleven," Drexel said.

"I was twenty-four," Mary said. "And in those last couple of years before she died I got to know Granny B a lot better. I would stay with her at night sometime, when it got to where she couldn't stay by herself. We would sit up late talking, and she told me a lot of stories."

"I don't suppose I really knew all that much about her life," Drexel said. "I was always more interested in looking at the pictures of Deputy Bryant and listening to the men talk about him."

"Well, Granny B had quite a life of her own," Mary said. "I'm going to tell you something that is going to shock you."

"What's that?"

"Before Sam and Mabel were married," Mary said, "Sam was already the deputy sheriff with a tough reputation. Mabel was his girlfriend. Also with a tough reputation. You had to be tough to make it in Coleman Springs back in those days. There were more saloons than churches, and about as many brothels as saloons." Mary took a deep breath. "Mabel ran one of the brothels."

"Granny B ran a ho . . . a house of ill repute?" Drexel exclaimed.

"Over on Third Street," Mary said. "It was a frame house that was torn down years ago."

"She told you this?"

"Yes, and she said I shouldn't talk about it. She didn't want people to remember her that way. And I haven't told anyone else other than Mac. But I thought you ought to know."

Mary laughed. "I didn't think you were old enough before. But now, Admiral, I suppose you are!"

Drexel shook his head in disbelief. "Granny B ran a ho . . . a brothel. For how long?"

"Oh, she said it was just for a few months. She and Sam had started living together, more or less, but Granny B—Mabel—said none of it felt right to her. That's not the way she had been raised and not the kind of life she had envisioned for herself. She just kind of drifted into it.

"One Sunday night there was a visiting evangelist in town and he was preaching down at the Baptist church. Mabel said something inside made her feel like she ought to go hear him. She said that when she walked in the church, people stared at her and she could tell they were whispering, 'What's she doing here?'

"But one woman stood and took her hand and asked Mabel if she would like to sit with her. Mabel said that little act of kindness made up for all the stares and whispers. She said she felt strangely at home, at peace.

"When the evangelist finished his sermon, Mabel was in tears. She walked down to the front, and her new friend went with her. Mabel fell on her knees and asked for forgiveness and was 'saved.'

"That night she went home and closed the brothel and told Sam that she couldn't live with him in sin anymore. If they were going to be together, they would have to get married. And he would need to go to church."

"What did he say?" Drexel asked.

"She said that Sam thought for a minute and said, 'Let's go see the preacher.' They went to the Baptist preacher's house and knocked on his door. It was very late. He came to the door, and Sam told him, 'Preacher, Mabel and I want to get married. Tonight.'

"The preacher got up and took them over to the church and married them that night. The next week Sam went down to the front and asked for forgiveness for his sins.

"Mabel said Sam didn't go to church all that often, but she said he was a changed man after that. Oh, he was still plenty tough. But mixed in with the toughness was a sense of fairness and a deep compassion for poor people. He was still the law, but it was tempered with mercy."

"What a story!" Drexel said. "Here we are sitting in your living room just a few blocks from where our grandmother operated a, uh, brothel."

"Yes," Mary said, "but the real story is not that, but what she did with the rest of her life. The home she and Sam built. The children they had—my father and your father. The influence Sam and Mary and our fathers had in this town. The influence you have had around the world. That's the story, Drexel. That's the story of grace and love. That's the story of our family. That's the story."

14

Bobo Kennedy

Bobo Kennedy came into the post office this morning and walked right up to the counter and said, "Mac, do you notice anything different about me?"

Well, yeah! His bobo was gone. Bobo was now bobo-less.

He has been Bobo for all sixty-one of his years up to now. Bobo was born Larry Kennedy, but Larry had a black mole about the size of a dime right in the middle of his forehead. His older brother, Bert, took one look at his baby brother and immediately dubbed him Bobo.

And Bobo it was, from that time on. It didn't seem to bother Bobo that everyone—except his mother and father—called him Bobo. That's just who he was. (His mom and dad shortened it to Bo.)

In high school Bobo became one of the most feared linebackers in the history of Coleman Springs Bandits football. His senior year he led the district in tackles, sacks, fumbles caused, fumbles recovered, punts blocked, and quarterbacks

psyched out. Four colleges offered him scholarships, but Bobo wasn't all that awesome in the classroom. He joined the Army instead.

In Vietnam he won a Silver Star and two Purple Hearts for his bravery. He came home and married Betsy Maguire and they had two sons and a daughter, and one of the sons became a well-known actor on TV. Bobo and Betsy have seven grandchildren now.

Betsy always called him Bo, not Bobo. And I suppose that's what the rest of us will call him now. Bo. Not Bobo. There's no bobo.

"I went to the doctor a couple of weeks ago for my annual physical," Bobo said. "For years he had been telling me I ought to have the mole removed, but I never seemed to have the time or the money, and I just let it go.

"This time he said we really needed to do something about it or it might become cancerous. That got my attention. I went in the next day and had it taken off. It didn't hurt or nothing, and I was home for supper.

"The funny thing is," he continued, "last weekend we were having the reunion of our district championship team. I talked to Coach Bennett for probably fifteen minutes, but later one of the guys came up to me and said, 'Coach Bennett was saying that he sure missed Bobo Kennedy and hoped he was coming to the reunion.' I said, 'I just talked to Coach for fifteen minutes a little while ago.' Obviously he didn't know who I was without the bobo."

Bobo Kennedy has been Bobo for sixty-one years. It seems strange to call him Bo, but not as strange as Larry. Obviously, he isn't Bobo anymore.

I suppose we will get used to "Bo" in time. Evidently he will be around for a while, and that's good. We need more guys like Bobo Kennedy, or Bo Kennedy, or Larry Kennedy, or whoever he is.

15

Zolly

People around here swear that Zolly Quivnik got his name from a Scrabble game. Zolly is from the "old country," wherever that is. No one is quite sure.

No one is quite sure of his age either. He's somewhere between fifty and seventy. I suspect closer to seventy, but who knows? I'm sure Zolly does, but he isn't telling. At least not so anyone can understand him.

Zolly came to Coleman Springs about five years ago, but no one knows why—or how. Just showed up one day and has been here ever since. He has no job, speaks with a heavy accent, pretty much keeps to himself. He doesn't drive a car and he lives in a small rent house.

He walks everywhere he goes, always dressed in a long-sleeved khaki shirt and khaki pants, even in the summer. Evidently he gets by on a check that comes in the mail around the first of every month.

He doesn't rent a post office box, so he doesn't come in very often to check his mail—and certainly not to visit.

Around the first of the month he comes to the front counter and we retrieve what little mail has come for him, addressed to General Delivery, Coleman Springs. I've tried to engage him in conversation, with no luck.

Luther Moore, who rents the house to Zolly, said he keeps the place tidy and always pays his rent on time. He has a little garden in the back yard—tomatoes, peas, squash, melon, and corn.

Luther said Zolly doesn't have a TV but apparently reads a lot because there is always a stack of books on the end table by his big chair.

The librarian, Miss Jenny Simpson, said Zolly comes in a couple of times a week and checks out four or five books each time. She didn't volunteer—and I didn't think it polite to inquire—as to what kinds of books he reads.

All of this is to say that Zolly Quivnik is one of those odd characters who probably exist in most towns and cities. In the larger cities, his behavior might not seem so peculiar, simply because he would just kind of blend in. In a small town like Coleman Springs everyone knows everyone, so someone like Zolly is noticed.

This morning Zolly was walking home from Bales Grocery & Drug carrying a small sack of groceries when Opal Landers ran her car head-on into a telephone pole and hit her head hard on the steering wheel.

Zolly was the first person at the scene. Mrs. Landers was unconscious and blood was gushing from a gash on her forehead. He gently picked her up and moved her out of the car, pulled a handkerchief out of his pocket and applied it to her head, checked her pulse made sure she was breathing all right, and sat with her until someone called Dr. Campbell and he came running over from his clinic, just a block away.

Once the doctor took over, Zolly stood up and walked off, his khaki shirt covered with blood. He didn't say a word to anybody, just picked up his sack of groceries and walked home.

The ladies from Mrs. Landers' Sunday school class at the Methodist church brought flowers to her hospital room and took turns sitting with her for a couple of days until she could be driven home.

When she got home, there was a basket of fresh tomatoes on her doorstep. There was no note—but we all know who brought them.

16

Pappy Died

My friend Taylor Campbell, our local doctor, came by early this morning. He didn't need anything—stamps or such—just needed to talk. He was almost in tears.

"I had to have Pappy put to sleep this morning," Taylor said.

No wonder he was so sad.

"Oh, I'm so sorry," I told Taylor. "I know how much you loved Pappy."

Someone overhearing our conversation might have been shocked if they didn't know that Pappy is Taylor's golden retriever. He's had Pappy more years than he's had his second wife, Jill.

"It just got to where Pappy couldn't function anymore," Taylor said. "Jill and I would put out food, and he would barely touch it. He just lay there, hardly moving.

"When he did go outside yesterday morning, he wouldn't come back in. Mac, I think he went outside to die.

We picked him up and carried him back in the house, but this morning he hadn't moved from where we laid him. He was barely breathing.

"I could tell he had been in pain for quite a while. I just couldn't bring myself to let him go. But this morning, I told Jill I was going to take him to Dr. Waters, the vet over in Walnut Cove, and have him put out of his misery. It just seemed like the humane thing to do.

"Dr. Waters—Will—was very sensitive. He said it would be better if I just let him handle it. I suppose I could have stayed with Pappy and held him, and I kind of wanted to, but Will thought it would best if I didn't. So I gave Pappy a kiss and then I cried. I sat outside in the waiting room.

"It didn't take long. Will wrapped up Pappy in a little blanket and put him in a cardboard box with a lid, like a coffin I suppose. Will gave me a hug and I carried Pappy's box out to the car.

"I went home and dug a grave and buried Pappy in the back yard. I don't think I'll put up a tombstone or anything, but somehow I feel better knowing that Pappy is still close by. I'll probably plant some wildflowers on his grave. I think he would like that."

Taylor was quiet for a moment. Neither of us said anything. Then he said, "Mac, I really appreciate the peaceful way in which Pappy died, and it certainly made me stop and think about how much more humane we are with our pets' final days than we are with the people we love.

"When my father had Alzheimer's, I know he wanted to go ahead and die. He even said so at one point before the Alzheimer's got so bad, and even after he couldn't talk

I know that he would have preferred to save himself and everyone else the misery of continuing to live with such a debilitating condition.

"Of course, we couldn't do for him what I did for Pappy. And I know there are all kinds of ethical and moral ramifications involving euthanasia, in addition to the legal issues, and I am sworn as a physician to view life as sacred. But Mac, I have to wonder, which is more humane, which is really more sacred in the long run—to let people continue to suffer when there is no hope for recovery or improvement, or to do what I did this morning with Pappy?"

"Taylor," I said, "I agree with you, but I doubt that is an issue you and I can decide here in Coleman Springs."

"I know, Mac," he said. "But maybe we at least ought to raise the questions. I'm going to write a letter to someone. I don't know who, and I doubt it will make any difference, but I will feel better getting my thoughts down on paper."

"You do that, Taylor," I said.

Later that day I sent a small check to the regional animal shelter in Pappy's name. That evening Mary and I talked about what Taylor had said.

"I would certainly rather go like Pappy did," Mary said.

"I would, too," I said, "but don't go getting any ideas!"

17

Postcard Minister

Lacy Curry sent another postcard to the President of the United States today.

Every few months she writes a postcard to the President. Not a protest or anything, and not necessarily agreeing with him either.

She just writes something like, "Dear Mr. President, You have a tough job, and I just want to say thank you."

Or, "Dear Mr. President, I will be praying for you."

Or, "Dear Mr. President, May you be blessed with wisdom and grace."

Or, "Dear Mr. President, We are counting on you."

Lacy has been sending postcards like that to the White House since Eisenhower was President. She has written them all, about four or five times a year on average, whether she voted for them or not.

It started with an English assignment when Lacy was in high school over in Crayton. The teacher handed out three

postcards to everyone in class and told them to write three people and say something encouraging to them.

Lacy chose her grandmother, who was barely able to see anymore, knowing someone would read it to her. Then she sent a card to a cousin, congratulating him on winning a blue ribbon for his trumpet solo. And then she decided to write President Eisenhower.

She was surprised to get a reply from the White House. So a couple of months later, she wrote him again, and every so often after that while he was in office. When Kennedy became President, she continued her little hobby. Then Johnson, Nixon, Ford, Carter, Reagan, and each one since. They've all written her back, just standard, official White House replies at first, but eventually each President wrote her a personal letter saying how much they looked forward to receiving her kind words of encouragement.

She never tried to sway any of their views on any issue, figuring, "They are there and they have a lot more information than I do. I just want them to know that someone cares and appreciates the often thankless job they have to do."

During Nixon's and Clinton's darkest days of investigation and impeachment hearings, she wrote messages like, "Dear Mr. President, May you have the strength to face these trying times." Or, "Dear Mr. President, May the Lord bless you and keep you all the day long."

Lacy moved here with her new husband, Bob, when Johnson was president. I got to know her right away, not just because she wrote to the president frequently, but also because she wrote a postcard to someone *every day*. At least one. You might say she has been one of my best customers through the years. I figure that she has probably sent fifteen to twenty thousand postcards in her lifetime. Or more.

Someone new moves to town, they get a postcard from Lacy welcoming them to Coleman Springs. When kids she knows go off to college, she sends them a postcard after about a month, thinking they might be getting a little homesick by then. Anyone in town who needs cheering up will get a postcard from Lacy.

She calls it her "postcard ministry."

"Mac," she said, "it's just a little thing, but it's a little thing that I can do."

Several years ago the Chamber of Commerce honored her as our Citizen of the Year. Appropriately, the next week, she received congratulatory postcards from nearly everyone in town.

18

★ ★ ★ ★ ★

A Poem for the Plumber

George Gibbons, the Official Poet Laureate of Coleman Springs, was holding a postcard in his hand when he stopped by the front counter.

"Mac," he said, "evidently not everyone in Coleman Springs appreciates great poetry."

I was shocked. Everyone that I know thinks the world of George Gibbons and his way with words.

He shook the postcard at me. But then he laughed.

"See, it started last week when the plumbing stopped up at our house. I called Lester, of course, to come out and fix it."

Lester is Lester Maybridge, the only plumber in Coleman Springs since Ike Landers died. In high school, Lester was a ferocious defensive back on the Bandits football team. He picked up the nickname Lester the Arrester. He stopped everything that came his way.

With a name like Lester the Arrester, you would think that Lester Maybridge would be a fan of fine rhyme.

Apparently that isn't so, at least according to George Gibbons.

"Well, I called Lester, and he called back on his cell phone and said he would try to get there that afternoon," George said. "He got there the next afternoon, about when I expected him, actually a day or two before I really *expected* him.

"Of course, he had to talk about his motorcycle and the latest rock concert he had attended and so on. All the while, I figure, the meter is running.

"Finally, he got around to trying to figure out the problem with my plumbing, and then he had to take awhile to analyze it and decide what needed to be done. The meter, I know, is still running.

"As a poet, I know something about meter, and so a poem began to formulate in my head. By the time he was finished, I had written Lester a poem. I called it 'An Ode to a Plumber,' and it went like this:

While you fixed my commode
I sat on my deck
And wrote you this ode—
As well as a check.

Maybe you'll deduct
A little this time
Since I took the trouble
To write you a rhyme.

$$G^2$$

"He didn't deduct anything, not that I expected him to," George said. "He took my check and talked for twenty more minutes about this and that. I should have been charging *him* by the hour!

"And then today, I get this," he added, waving the postcard.

I remembered that Lester came in with a postcard yesterday and bought a stamp. I put it in George's box but didn't read it, of course.

George handed me the postcard, which contained just four lines:

Your check was good
(I'm in a rush)
Call me again
When you can't flush.
    Lester

"So now everyone's a poet," George said. "I suppose I'll have to take up plumbing."

To which I replied:

Yes, there are some
poets who plumb,
but those who do
soon tire of poo.

George just shook his head and walked out the door.

19

Payback Time

Across the square, I could see Pete Harwood walking with a purpose toward the library.

Pete is president of Coleman Springs State & National Bank, a big man in town and a big man, period. Pete was an offensive lineman at Princeton and then went on to get his MBA at Northwestern and marry the banker's daughter from Coleman Springs.

He and Heather had a big wedding here, then he went to work at the bank. Within three years he was vice president and five years later was president. Now he's president and CEO, which means his father-in-law, J. Robert Thomason, has finally put him completely in charge. J. Robert and his wife, Suzy, moved to their lake home.

Anyway, there was Pete Harwood walking briskly into the library. Out of the corner of my eye, I also noticed that Morris Jenkins, who owns Coleman Springs Hardware, was just kind of standing on the sidewalk observing.

A few minutes later, Pete walked out of the library, a lot more casually, carrying one book. I had to wonder what was going on.

Pete is well liked around town. He has a booming voice and a hearty laugh. He's known as a great practical joker. He isn't known, however, as a great reader. So why was he walking out of the library carrying a book?

Morris Jenkins supplied the answer a little later. He was laughing so hard he could barely speak. And he made me promise I wouldn't tell, which I haven't (until now).

Morris is Pete's next door neighbor, and Pete is always playing practical jokes on Morris. One of his best ones was when Pete learned that Morris had brought home a popcorn machine to try out before putting it in his store.

Morris thought he would have a few of his kids' friends over and pop a little corn so he could see how it worked. Then he could sell popcorn at the hardware store and pick up a little extra money. When you run a store in a small town, every dollar counts.

Morris made the mistake of telling Pete about the popcorn machine. Pete secretly had signs printed up and hired a couple of teenagers to put them in yards all over town.

FREE POPCORN

1324 LEXINGTON

ANYTIME DAY OR NIGHT

JUST RING THE DOORBELL

Morris didn't get any sleep that night. The doorbell started ringing a little before supper and continued all night. When he would go to the door, it was the same message, "We're here for the free popcorn."

Morris didn't want to offend anyone, since everyone in town was a potential customer, so all night he handed out bags of freshly popped corn.

Shortly before eleven, when he was giving six bags to the Pernfors family, he noticed Pete Harwood watching from his driveway next door. Pete was grinning, and Morris figured out that somehow Pete must be behind this.

The next day driving to work, Morris saw a few of the signs, and then he knew for sure.

"Somehow, someway," Morris vowed, "I will get even."

That was several months ago. Late last night, Pete came over and told Morris he needed to talk to him about something. In private.

Pete was kind of hesitant, almost shy, which wasn't like Pete.

"Uh, Morris," Pete said, "I'm having some constipation problems. I haven't been able to go to the bathroom for two days."

"Oh, I know just the thing that will take care of it," Morris said. He was serious. He recommended a laxative that would take care of the problem in about twelve hours. He even had a couple of extra pills he could give him. "Just take these and go to work and before noon you should get plenty of relief."

Pete was so thankful. He took the pills with him and went back to his house.

That's when the idea hit Morris. Payback time!

The next morning, Morris got to the bank before Pete did. He was carrying a flight bag. Inside the flight bag was a pair of high-topped boots.

Morris went into the men's room at the bank. The men's room, as Morris knew, has a couple of urinals and one private stall with a door. There is a ten-inch gap between the bottom of the stall door and the floor.

Morris pulled out the pair of high-topped boots and placed them in the stall so it would appear occupied. He then locked the stall door and slid out under the door.

About ten o'clock that morning, Morris figured that the laxatives should be taking effect. He thought it would be a good time to go over to transact some business.

He watched as Pete walked briskly from his office to the men's room. Seconds later, Pete walked back out, a pained look on his face.

This happened two more times within the next fifteen minutes while Morris found excuses to take care of other bank business. He checked his checking account balance. He checked his savings balance. He looked over the documents in his safety deposit box.

Pete was in pain, Morris could tell, and Morris was enjoying every minute of it.

Finally, when Pete went to the men's room for the fourth time, he came out and headed straight for the library, where there is a public restroom. Pete was walking with a purpose. Morris went outside and watched one more time, then went back to his hardware store satisfied that he had finally gotten even.

Of course, Pete had to check out a book to make his quick trip to the library look legitimate.

I don't know what the book was about, and it probably didn't matter to Pete. The next day, however, Pete received a post card in the mail at his house. It read:

"Thank you for your patronage of the Coleman Springs Public Library. We hope you enjoyed your visit and will come see us again when the urge hits you."

The card was unsigned.

20

The Love Sermon

The Presbyterians were all abuzz today about C. J. Fletcher's "Love Sermon" yesterday.

Most really liked it, but some didn't. Those who didn't like it felt it just wasn't substantive enough. After all it lasted, what, maybe two or three minutes at the most?

Presbyterians are used to longer sermons, though not as long as Baptist sermons. But every now and then, Dr. Fletcher preaches a very short sermon—just a few lines. I think he does it to get our attention. I mean, how many times have you heard anyone complain that a preacher's sermon was *too* short?

Well, you can judge for yourself.

When it came time for the sermon, C. J. didn't even step up to the pulpit. Instead, he stood on the second step of the rostrum for maybe thirty seconds without saying anything. Finally, he looked at the families on his left and spoke.

"Love," he said.

76

He paused, then faced the parishioners clustered in the center aisles.

"Love."

Another pause. He looked to his right, where several members sat.

"Love."

Turning from left to right as he spoke each word very slowly, he continued.

"God . . . is . . . love . . .

"God . . . is . . . love.

Pause.

"Love God.

"Love yourself.

"Love others."

Pause.

"Love more.

"Love well.

"Love deeply."

Another pause.

"Love goodness.

"Love joy.

"Love life."

For what seemed like a full minute he looked at the mesmerized worshippers, who now hung on every word.

"God is love," he said.

"Go with God."

Then he sat down.

Jason Turnbull, father of three and a young deacon at the church, came by this morning and said that when they got home, his family spent more than an hour at lunch and after lunch talking about the "Love Sermon" and what it meant to their family.

"We've never spent five minutes before talking about any sermon," he said.

"You call that a sermon?" said Ida Frazier when she stopped by to mail a package.

"Well, Ida, I rather liked it!" her friend Margie Blanchard pitched in. "He got right to the point, didn't he? We ought to love more. Isn't that what we should be doing?"

Ida didn't seem to have a comeback to that.

"Mac," Margie said, "when was the last time people came in here talking about a preacher's sermon?"

"Well, not since C. J.'s last short sermon," I said. "You know, a couple of months ago."

"That's my point," Margie said. "I bet we have more people in church next Sunday to see what he might say next."

I wouldn't be surprised.

21

★ ★ ★ ★ ★

Galindo's Romance

The mail in Galindo Vazquez's mailbox has been piling up, and I was getting a little worried. Galindo comes by at least every other day to check his mail. I hadn't seen him in a couple of weeks.

Today he came in, and he looked great.

"Mac," he said, "I got married."

I was speechless, which is rare for me. Galindo Vazquez is quite possibly the ugliest man in Coleman Springs. Certainly among the top three.

A nice guy, to be sure, one of the nicest. But when it comes to looks, look somewhere else.

"I know what you're thinking," Galindo said. "Who would marry this ugly mug?"

Finally, I recovered enough to talk. "Well, congratulations, Galindo. I can't think of anyone more deserving. Tell me all about it."

"I don't know if you remember, but a few weeks ago I got a letter telling me I had won a vacation to Las Vegas," Galindo said.

"Yes, I do remember," I said. "It was from one of those casinos, wasn't it?"

"It was. I thought, well, why not? I haven't had a vacation in years. So I called the 800 number and signed up.

"They sent me a plane ticket, and when I got to the airport in Las Vegas, they had a limousine waiting for me. I haven't been treated this well since I got the game ball for kicking the field goal that won the game against West Central."

I remembered that, of course. Everyone in town does. West Central was ahead 21-20 with three seconds to go, and the Bandits were at the West Central thirty-one-yard-line. Coach Davenport sent Galindo in to try a field goal.

It was a desperation move, at best. This was a forty-eight-yard kick, and Galindo hadn't kicked one any longer than thirty yards all year. Even the short ones were a challenge for him.

The snap was perfect. The hold was perfect. Galindo kicked the ball with all his might. And missed it. Not even close. Oh, well, it was a good try.

But wait, there was a flag. One of the rushers had run into Galindo after the kick. The ball was moved to the sixteen-yard-line. Now it was a thirty-three-yard kick, almost within Galindo's range.

The Bandits lined up. The snap was high, but the holder got the ball down, and Galindo nailed it. We won 23-21.

His teammates lifted Galindo on their shoulders and carried him off the field. He was given the game ball. It was the high point of his life.

Until now.

"I want you meet the new Mrs. Vazquez, Rhoda Vazquez," Galindo said.

On cue, Rhoda Vazquez walked through the door. She was absolutely one of the most gorgeous women I've ever seen. But when she spoke, it sounded like fingernails on a blackboard.

"HOW DO YOU DO, MAC?" she said. "GALINDO HAS TOLD ME SO MUCH ABOUT YOU."

I managed to say, "Welcome to Coleman Springs, Mrs. Vazquez."

"Mac," Galindo said, "we met at the one-dollar slot machine at the Desert Majestic. Rhoda had been playing the slots and hadn't won a thing. I came up and she said, 'WISH ME LUCK, HONEY,' and I said, 'Well, good luck, sweetheart,' and she hit the jackpot. I mean THE jackpot. It spit out silver dollars for ten or fifteen minutes. They said it was the most money anyone had ever won at that slot machine."

"WE WERE MARRIED AN HOUR LATER," Rhoda said. "THEY GAVE US A **FREE** HONEYMOON SUITE, AND LET ME TELL YOU, GALINDO VAZQUEZ IS THE **MAN** OF MY DREAMS."

"I told her I would only marry her if we could live in Coleman Springs," Galindo said.

"AND I SAID, ARE YOU **KIDDING**? I'VE **ALWAYS** WANTED TO LIVE IN COLEMAN SPRINGS!" Rhoda said.

Rhoda smiled. Galindo smiled.

Well, you just never know, do you?

22

A Wonderful Life

Our town is different today. People are going about their daily routine, but it is as if a cloud has descended and we are all in a daze or a fog. There is no laughter, no joy, no small talk. It doesn't seem appropriate.

When tragedy strikes a small town, where everyone knows everyone else, it affects the entire town. No one is immune. We all feel the pain.

We know we will be a long time recovering. Life in Coleman Springs will never be quite the same. Eventually, we suppose, life will resume its normal pace and people will smile again and will find meaning and purpose in what we do. But it will not be the same.

We all want to say something, we want to do something, we want to make some sense of it and give our friends some relief from the overwhelming sorrow that surrounds and penetrates and engulfs them.

And, like our friends, we want to remember. We cling to the idea that life is a gift and we remember that the candle, which has been snuffed out so abruptly, burned so brightly and illuminated our lives, even if ever so briefly.

Rainey McDermond was, without question, the most beautiful girl in her class when she graduated from Coleman Springs High School fifteen years ago. She had a natural beauty that needed no artificial enhancement. She did not flaunt it; if anything, she did all she could to play down the fact of how gorgeous she really was.

As a child she was quite the tomboy. She liked to collect frogs and lizards and rocks, go fishing in Blue Pond, organize neighborhood camp-outs in her back yard, and challenge all the boys to a foot race which she knew she would win.

But there was no hiding the fact, especially when she entered high school, that she was beautiful. And her smile and her laugh and her easy-going charm drew people to her. She made friends easily, and she made friends abundantly.

Not just among her peers either. Old men and women, and little girls and boys, and parents of her high school pals, found themselves drawn like a magnet into her circle.

No wonder she was voted not only most beautiful, but most likely to succeed. She went off to college, majored in elementary education, taught second grade, married a young preacher in North Carolina, and gave birth to two beautiful children—a daughter, with red hair like her mother, and a son who, it quickly became apparent, had inherited his mother's athletic ability.

And then, about a year ago, during a routine exam the doctor found a lump. And then another and another. The doctors did everything they could, but in the end there wasn't anything left to do.

Rainey and her husband prayed like they had never prayed before. When it became apparent that their prayers would not be answered in the way they had hoped, they began making plans for life for the family after she was gone.

Her parents, Kevan and Paige McDermond, were devastated. They went to North Carolina to be with their daughter and to help with the grandchildren. Friends in Coleman Springs sent cards and letters and numerous prayers their way. A fund was organized to help with medical costs.

Rainey fought with everything she had. "Every day," she told her mother, "is a gift from God. I know you have taught me that all my life, but now I see it more clearly and feel it more deeply."

She was in and out of the hospital several times. Finally, the last time, she knew it was the last time. She asked her dad to go to her favorite bakery and buy a big chocolate cake. And then she threw one last party for the nurses and aides and doctors who had been so kind to her.

That was a week ago Friday. She held on for three more days and said all her good-byes. She told her husband, "I am the luckiest woman in the world to have been married to you and to have had two wonderful children. I have truly had, as the movie said, a wonderful life. Thank you."

They had the funeral at their church in North Carolina but also held a memorial service for her at the Baptist church here. Her husband spoke briefly, and so did her father and one of her friends from high school. The congregation sang, at her request, "When We All Get to Heaven."

The Rev. Andrew Baker got up to deliver a sermon, but, instead of speaking, he had us stand and hold hands and sing "Blest Be the Tie." Everyone was hugging, crying, remembering, and praying.

And two days later, we still are.

23

Pop Ellison

Pop Ellison just walked by. For the third time.

Now he will sit awhile on the bench in the little park behind the post office. Then he will walk around the square two more times, smiling and waving every time he walks by.

He does that every morning about the time we open. He doesn't come inside, just walks by and waves. Five times. Then he walks home.

You can't miss Pop. He dresses, uh, let's say, rather colorfully. Today, for example, he was wearing yellow shorts held up with a black dress belt, cinched tightly at least eight inches above his actual waistline. He had on a white T-shirt with bright red letters proclaiming, "World's Greatest Grandpa." His brown socks were pulled up to mid-calf, with black Velcro athletic shoes. He was wearing an orange Baltimore Orioles baseball cap.

If Pop is walking across the street, his garb stops traffic. And that's the point. Kind of.

Pop came here a couple of years ago to live with his daughter, Diane Gorman, and her husband, Blake, and their two daughters. Pop's wife, Merinda, had died, and Pop just wasn't able to cope. Diane suggested he move in with them.

"We have plenty of room, Pop," she said. "And you will love Coleman Springs."

Pop is eighty or so. He retired at least fifteen years ago. A partner in a big-city accounting firm, he parted his name in the middle back then—J. Robert Ellison. Those who worked with him called him J. Robert. Not Jay. Not Bob. Certainly not Pop.

J. Robert was all business, Diane told me—suit, white shirt, tie every day. He made a lot of money, but at home it was Merinda—Mom—who ran the house. She had taste and style. She cooked. She paid the bills. She took care of the kids. She made everything work.

When J. Robert retired, he and Merinda traveled some. But then Merinda got very sick and for several years she had to live in a nursing facility before she finally passed away. Pop moved into the same room so he could be with her, could sit by her bedside, read to her, hold her hand, talk to her, feed her, call the nurse's station when she needed help.

After she was gone, he was lost. So Diane invited him to come live with them in Coleman Springs.

Now, every morning, he gets up and gets dressed. Not in a suit, white shirt, and tie, but in his "walking clothes," his casual attire. And it certainly gets interesting.

"Mom always picked out his clothes when he was working," Diane said. "But I don't do that. I let him pick them out himself, and I just stand back and marvel that anyone could have such impeccably poor taste!"

But there's a good side to it, she said.

"I don't have to worry about someone running over him."

Every morning when he leaves, she kisses his cheek and says, "Have a nice walk, Pop " She knows everyone will wave to him and watch out for him.

24

★ ★ ★ ★ ★

A Tie at Work

I wear a coat and tie to work every day. In the summer I may hang up the coat, but I always keep on the tie.

You don't see many men wearing ties in Coleman Springs. Maybe four or five on an average day, unless there's a funeral in town. Most people still dress up for funerals, although it's not quite as common as it used to be.

For me, wearing a tie makes me feel like I'm at work. It just seems more businesslike, more professional I suppose. I'm afraid if I wasn't wearing a tie, I might forget where I am. And, after all these years, people would talk. "Hey, did you see Mac isn't wearing a tie? Wonder what's the matter?" The tie is part of my uniform, part of my personality. Mac Spearman wears a tie to work.

The president of the bank, Pete Harwood, wears a tie nearly every day, except casual Fridays, when bank employees are allowed to dress more casually than usual, including jeans. No shorts, however. On casual Fridays, the president wears starched jeans or pressed slacks and an expensive golf shirt. Frankly, I think he looks more uncomfortable, more unnatural in his "casual" clothes than he does in a coat and tie. And that's how I would feel, too.

The only other men in town who consistently wear ties are Brother Baker, the Baptist preacher, and C. J. Fletcher, the Presbyterian preacher, and Jameson Pratt, the new young math teacher at the high school. The preachers you can understand. But Jameson Pratt is a surprise. He's only twenty-seven or twenty-eight, at the most, and you really don't see a lot of young men these days who wear ties. Not that many old ones either, for that matter, but especially not young ones.

Since we have that in common, Jameson and I got to talking about it.

"Mac," he said, "you know, I don't have to wear a tie. None of the other men teachers do, not even the principal most of the time unless he's meeting with the school board or something. I just feel a little more 'on' when I'm in a tie."

"Me, too," I said. "I'm not trying to impress anybody by wearing a tie. I'm certainly not trying to make a fashion statement. It's just that when I have on a tie, I feel ready to do business. As soon as I get home, I take it off. The business day is over."

Jameson Pratt's ties are a lot flashier than mine. Mine are not very bold—solids, a few diagonal stripes, some conservative patterns. Jameson goes in for a little more color, bolder stripes, even vertical and horizontal stripes, polka dots, pinks and greens and purples.

"Well," he explained, "wearing a tie makes me feel grown up. Wearing bright colors and vivid patterns reminds me that I'm still young."

He buys most of his ties from a tie shop in Granger Falls and gets some by mail order. Today he came by and brought me one.

"Now, Mac, this might be a little out on the edge for you," he said. "But see what you think."

It was a silk tie with thin red and white horizontal stripes about a quarter of an inch wide. It was so "not me." I loved it.

"It will be great for all kinds of occasions," I said, "especially around Christmas and Valentine's. Or any other time I want to feel a little younger." I took off the navy blue tie I was wearing and put on the red and white striped tie. Pretty handsome, if I say so myself!

He had enclosed a card, showing a woman pulling a man by his tie toward her. Under the woman's caricature he had penciled in "(Mary)." Inside he wrote, "Mac, tie one on! Jameson."

I'm sure Mary won't be able to resist me when she sees me in my new tie. Well, maybe she can.

25

Wendy Weather

Her name is Wendy, and wouldn't you know it, she would grow up and marry Preston Day. That made her Wendy Day, and of course she has taken a lot of ribbing about her name over the years.

"Windy day, isn't it, Wendy," is the sort of thing she hears a lot. Even more so in the last couple of years.

So when she decided to go back to college and finish her degree, what did she major in but meteorology? With a name like Wendy Day, she figured she might as well make the most of it.

Besides, she had always enjoyed studying the weather. When she was a girl here in Coleman Springs—Wendy Stanton back then—she won the science fair one year for her exhibit on tornadoes. She told how to watch for them and what to do if you see one coming.

It turned out to be more than a prize-winning entry. It probably saved the life of one of the science fair judges who,

a few weeks later, encountered a tornado and, remembering Wendy's advice, steered his family to safety. He wrote and thanked her.

Now that Wendy has finished her degree, she has been hired by one of the TV stations in Granger Falls as their weekend weather forecaster. She and Preston and their two children still live in Coleman Springs, so Wendy commutes the thirty-two miles in to work, but just on the weekends.

She usually signs off her forecasts with "Have a good day. Wendy Day reporting." With her smile and her professional demeanor, she has proven to be so popular with viewers that the station really wants her to become its weekday weather person. But that would be more of a job commitment than Wendy is willing to make at this point in her life.

As a TV personality, Wendy has become quite a celebrity around Coleman Springs. The other day when she was in the post office to pick up her mail, the two little daughters of Brandi Hawkins ran up to her and asked for her autograph.

Wendy smiled and pulled out her pen and signed the back of her business card. "Have a good day! Wendy Day."

Last weekend we had a lot of flooding in our area. Several towns were hit hard by drenching rain and rising rivers, and Wendy stayed at the station reporting on the situation and letting people know which flooded streets to avoid.

She couldn't even drive home because water covered the major highway to Coleman Springs.

She called Preston on her cell phone to make sure he and the children were all right, then drove over to one of the shelters and helped serve meals to the flood victims who were spending the night there.

One elderly couple particularly caught her eye. They had lived in their home for more than forty years and had never been flooded before. Before they left, they grabbed up a stack of scrapbooks, the old man's stamp collection he had inherited from his father, their checkbook, and several jars of the woman's peach preserves.

"Sure would hate to see those preserves go to waste," the man smiled.

Wendy was impressed with their optimism.

"We're so much better off than most people," the woman said. "We have each other, and we've been able to save the things that were most valuable to us."

Wendy asked if they planned to go stay with family members until the flood subsided and their home could be repaired.

They have a daughter and son-in-law in another state, but "we haven't been able to get in touch with them yet," the man said. "We had to leave so fast and all."

Wendy pulled out her cell phone and offered to call for them.

The man on the other end answered.

"What is this," he said, "a joke?" It was well after midnight, after all.

"Uh, no sir," Wendy said.

"Well, my caller ID shows this call is from Wendy Day."

Wendy laughed and explained the situation.

"Are you with the Red Cross?" he asked.

"No," said Wendy. She didn't figure the man would believe her if she told him what she really did for a living. She just handed the phone to the old couple and went to get them another cup of coffee.

26

★ ★ ★ ★ ★

Miss Effie

Miss Effie Forrester taught third grade for more than fifty years. She was tough, but she wasn't mean, even though a lot of kids thought she was.

She made sure that when we finished her class we could read at third-grade level, at least, and we could add and subtract three-digit numbers. She even sneaked in some times tables, even though we really weren't supposed to get to that until fourth grade.

If we finished our work early, Miss Effie would send us to the blackboard (it really was black back then) and give us problems to work or words to spell. We didn't have "advanced placement" as such, but if you were in Miss Effie's class you knew that she expected more than just average.

People have been coming by all week to mail birthday cards to Miss Effie. Next week is her one hundredth birthday, and I can tell you she will be flooded with cards at the nursing home in Granger Falls.

Miss Effie lived here for a long time after she retired. Once a year she would come by and bring me a plate of cookies. There's a story behind that.

When I was in her class, one day right after Easter my mother packed a cookie in my sack lunch. That day I was so hungry that I couldn't wait until lunchtime. When Miss Effie's back was turned, I reached into my sack and pinched off a piece of my cookie.

Just as I was crunching it, Miss Effie turned around.

"Mac," she said, "what are you eating?"

"Nothing, Miss Effie," I said.

She walked over and looked at me. I reached in the sack and handed her the rest of the cookie.

"Well, Mac," she said, "you know you don't eat in my class."

She sent me to the blackboard and gave me seven really tough words to spell. I got every one of them right.

"One more," she said. "And if you get this one, I will bake you a plate of cookies myself."

Everyone in class sat up and paid attention.

Miss Effie knew I wouldn't be able to spell it.

"The word is 'indigestible.'"

I thought, there's no way I can spell such a long word. Then I started breaking it up into little parts.

"I-N" I paused. "D-I-G-E-S-T."

Uh-oh. Was it "A" or "I"? I closed my eyes and guessed. "I-B-L-E. Indigestible."

Miss Effie gave me that look that she gave us when we had done something wrong. I knew I had spelled it wrong.

After what seemed like five minutes, she said, "Mac, what is your favorite kind of cookie?"

"Chocolate chip," I said.

The next week she brought cookies for me, and for the rest of the class. And for nearly sixty years, until she went to the nursing home, every year right after Easter she would show up with a plate of cookies and a note: "I hope you don't find this indigestible! Love, Miss Effie."

Like nearly everyone else in town, I sent her a birthday card this week. But I also included a tin filled with chocolate chip cookies.

And a note.

"Happy Birthday, Miss Effie. These cookies may be indigestible, especially at your age! Love, Mac."

27

Simon's Secret

I could see Simon Pritchert coming up the sidewalk to the post office several minutes before he finally came in the door. Simon moves pretty slow, and not just because he is getting on up in years. Simon has always moved pretty slow.

Simon and Madge live about six miles out of town in the Oak Grove community, which isn't much of a community anymore. Years ago there was an elementary school at Oak Grove, but it's been closed for forty years or more. About all that's left of Oak Grove is the Oak Grove Cemetery and the Oak Grove Community Church, where Simon and Madge are faithful members and Simon sings a hearty bass during their fourth Sunday night hymn singing every month.

On Sundays Simon dresses up in his best black jeans, which Madge starches and irons, and a crisp white shirt, but no tie. The rest of the time you'll find Simon dressed in blue overalls with a blue work shirt. Two or three cigars are nearly always protruding out of the top pocket of the overalls.

Simon is probably five foot nine and weighs at least 275 pounds, and he's about out of breath by the time he makes it to my counter.

"How're you doing, Simon?" I always say.

He always has the same response, "'bout average, Mac."

Then he buys one book of first-class stamps, and always says, "Make sure they're purty ones. You know Madge likes the purty ones."

Simon and Madge get rural mail delivery, but about once a month he comes in for stamps. And, I know, for something else.

Simon farms a sizable piece of land. Well, that is to say he supervises his hired hand, Manuel, who actually does the work. Manuel and his wife Elena and their daughter Gina live in a little house on the farm, down a dirt road from Simon and Madge. Elena takes care of the Pritcherts' home and cooks for them.

"How are Manuel and Elena?" I ask.

"'bout average," says Simon.

Simon and Madge have a daughter, Bess, who teaches school in St. Louis, and she gets back here—like most of our kids who have moved away—two or three times a year.

There's nothing "'bout average" about Bess. Not that Simon is one to brag. Bess was valedictorian of Coleman Springs High School and earned an academic scholarship to Duke, then took an inner city teaching job. She was the school's Teacher of the Year four or five years ago.

Folks were a bit surprised how someone so average as Simon (and Madge, for that matter) could produce such a bright child. Well, the fact of the matter is that Simon really isn't average at all. You couldn't tell from looking at him, but he has one of the highest IQs of anyone around here. Doesn't talk much, but he thinks a lot.

And there's another facet of Simon that most people don't know. He and Madge are quietly generous. Besides their church, they send checks to several children's homes and children's hospitals. As Madge told me one time, "We're just so thankful for Bess that we wanted to help some other children who might need it."

After he buys his stamps, Simon always reaches in his pocket and hands me a hundred-dollar bill.

"You know what it's for, Mac," he says.

Yes I do. And I promised him years ago that I would pass it along and wouldn't tell a soul.

"See ya, Simon," I tell him.

Simon waves and begins the long, slow walk back to his truck.

28

Come Home

Typically, things don't happen very fast around Coleman Springs. We're kind of laid back here, you might say. Progress is measured in inches, perhaps centimeters.

But every once in a while, something grabs hold of folks and just takes off. That happened this week.

It started, as good things often do, with Cindi Timms. I mean, Cindi Phillips, her married name. Cindi, our former mayor, decided that Coleman Springs needed to do something to attract our young people back here to live. Like most small towns, we have a problem with that. Kids grow up here but are wooed by the opportunities, the high salaries, and the bright lights of the big city.

After a while, some of them come to see that the cost of living and the stress of city traffic and crime are not worth the extra money they make at higher-paying city jobs, and they yearn for the simpler times and calmer schedule of small town life.

Cindy thinks we should pursue our advantages more aggressively. For one thing, the cost of buying a home in Coleman Springs is a lot less than in the city. What if, she said, we played on that?

She pitched the idea to several friends, and the next thing you knew she had formed a new group called Come Home to Coleman Springs.

Anyone who graduated from high school in Coleman Springs would be able to buy or build a home here for no down payment and no house payments for the first year.

A free year of housing! When you're young and struggling to raise a family on a starting salary, or even two starting salaries, housing makes up a big percentage of the budget. Now here comes Coleman Springs with an offer of, essentially, free house payments for a year. And families would have their own home, not an apartment or a rented condo.

The bank jumped in with its support. Cindi's husband, Jacob, a home builder, figured out a way to make it happen.

The program, Come Home to Coleman Springs, was announced at a press conference on Monday and got media coverage in Granger Falls and all over the area. The next day two couples signed up. Two more signed up on Wednesday, another one on Thursday, one more on Friday. Eleven more couples with ties to Coleman Springs asked for information.

Thirty-six couples with no apparent connection to Coleman Springs asked if they could apply. Right now, Cindi said, the offer is only for those who want to "come home." But, she made it clear, the program might be expanded in the near future. She put their names on a waiting list.

Six new families already and the possibility of several more! Let's say in a year we get fifteen to twenty families to relocate here, with their one-point-five children. That would be a six to eight percent increase in population. Most of these families would be making good money working in Granger Falls while sending their children to our schools, paying property and sales taxes, shopping here, having their hair cut here, getting their mail here, supporting churches and charities here.

The point is, as all of us know but Cindi Phillips was able to articulate, small towns need to take advantage of what we have to offer. Especially towns like Coleman Springs that are close enough to the city to provide affordable housing and reasonable commuting distances.

Come Home to Coleman Springs. I really like the sound of it.

29

How Do You Spell 'Literacy'?

When it comes to math, we old-timers may not be much of a match for the young 'uns. Well, new math anyway.

But this wasn't math. It was the Coleman Springs Spell Off.

It was Janelle Perry's idea, and then she recruited Bambi Pearson, an avid reader, and Emily Pernfors. Together, they became the founding members of the Coleman Springs Literacy Council.

Everyone seemed to think it was a good idea to have a literacy council that would promote reading and writing. Goodness knows, we need more literacy these days.

Janelle Perry came up with the Coleman Springs Spell Off as a way to call attention to the issue—literacy—and to raise a little money to fund the cause. The idea was to take three fifth graders at Coleman Springs Elementary School

and put them up against three Coleman Springs adults in the first annual Coleman Springs Spell Off.

People would pay money for such a confrontation, Janelle figured. And she was right.

The event would be held on the stage of the elementary school, giving the kids the "home court advantage," I suppose. Admission was $2 per person. No one got in free, not even the spellers, of whom I was one. Several businesses paid to sponsor the event, including Bambi's Comb Aplomb beauty salon, the Coleman Springs Steak House, and the bank.

Way back there, more years ago than I care to admit, I won the Coleman Springs Spelling Bee. I was only in the fourth grade. The year before, as a third-grader, I came in second, which shocked everyone except my teacher, Miss Effie. All the next year I studied words and when the Spelling Bee came around, I waltzed through every round, winning handily.

And that was it. Even though I was eligible to compete again as a fifth-grader, I felt that I had nothing left to prove in the spelling department. I moved on to basketball and let someone else be the spelling champion.

Still, I always prided myself on being a good speller. So, when Janelle Perry asked if I would be a member of the adult team for the Coleman Springs Spell Off, I readily agreed. The other members were Claire Fletcher, the preacher's wife and a former spelling champ, and Simon Pritchert, the slow-moving, slow-talking genius farmer.

The three fifth graders chosen were all girls—the Steckham twins, Marti and Mandi, and Annabelle Coleman,

Evan Coleman's daughter. They had won an in-house spelling competition at the elementary school.

More than two hundred people gathered at the elementary school auditorium for the Spell Off. The team of fifth-graders wore white Fifth Grader t-shirts. The team of adults wore gray t-shirts proclaiming Been Around for a Spell.

A few side bets were placed, I understand. Pete Harwood bet on us, while Morris Jenkins sided with the kids. I figured it was a good sign when Jameson Pratt, the young math teacher at the high school, bet on us against Preston Day. Certainly it was reassuring to hear that the Poet Laureate of Coleman Springs, George Gibbons, had wagered on our behalf against Pierce Brock, the singing barber.

Obviously, the fifth-graders should be favored. They had just won a spelling competition at their school. They had been studying and practicing for months. And they were, after all, young.

Well, we would see about that.

The teams took the stage. The caller for the spelling match would be Miss Jenny Simpson, the city librarian. Miss Simpson explained the rules. In the first three rounds, one member from each team would be the designated speller per round, with all three having an opportunity to spell. In the fourth through seventh rounds, team members would be allowed to consult with each other before deciding on how to spell the given word. A team could ask to have the word used in a sentence. Once a speller began spelling a word into the microphone, he or she could not start over.

The words would be written on a placard and displayed to the audience so they would know whether the spellers were right. A team of three judges would have the final say.

The first round pitted Claire Fletcher against Mandi Steckham. Mandi went first.

Miss Simpson called out the word, "sandwich." Mandi smiled and spelled, "s-a-n-w-i-c-h." You could almost hear the crowd gasp, and Mandi covered her face, realizing her mistake.

Now it was Claire's turn. Miss Simpson called out "prophetic." Claire, the preacher's wife, spelled it correctly. One-oh.

I took the microphone for the second round. My word was "prosaic." I spelled it right. Marti Beckham's turn. She spelled "every." Two-one, us.

Annabelle Coleman spelled "touch." Two-two. Simon Pritchert was given "cholesterol." Not a problem. Three-two, us.

Now to the team spelling. We didn't stumble on "omniphibious," putting us up four-two. The Fifth Graders spelled "history." Four-three.

It was about then that the crowd discerned that the Been Around for a Spell team was, perhaps, getting harder words.

Fifth round. They went first: "computer." Well, that was easy. Four-four. Our word was "inimically." We each wrote it down and came up with three different answers. We went with mine, but unfortunately I had it "enemically."

Sixth round. We're first. Miss Simpson called out "heliotropism." None of us had any idea what it meant, but it didn't sound like a trick word, so we spelled it out phonetically and all came up with the right spelling. Five-four.

The Fifth Graders, appropriately, were given "softball." They knocked it out of the park. Five-five going into the last round.

For the seventh round, Miss Simpson decided that she had been kind enough to the kids. This time they got "epidemiologist." They froze. Finally, they offered a spelling that had a few of the right letters, but not anywhere near the right order.

Our turn. Miss Simpson smiled. Our word would be "auxiliary." If we spelled it right, we would win. We wrote it down and, again, had three spellings. I had it "auxillary." Claire had it "auxilliary." Simon got it right, "auxiliary," but wasn't all that sure. So we went with Claire, figuring she had been in more auxiliaries than we had. Wrong.

Overtime. We had to go first. Our word was "extraordinaire." All three of us had the same spelling. We were right. Six-five.

Miss Simpson lobbed one at the kids: "sell." They all smiled and scribbled down their spelling, without bothering to ask the caller to use the word in a sentence, which they were allowed to do.

Annabelle pulled the phone out of her pocket, waved it, and confidently spelled into the microphone, "c-e-l-l."

The audience sat in stunned silence. The three judges sadly shook their heads.

We had won on a trick word. No doubt there will be demands for a rematch.

30

Flash

Flash Robinson came by to say hello. He always does when he's in town, which isn't all that often.

Flash has gone by "Flash" since he was ten years old. You might think it is because of that big, wide smile he flashed back then, and still does today. But that's not it.

It goes back to the season I coached him in Little League. Actually I was just one of the assistant coaches, helping out with the Cardinals. My own son, Bryant, was the catcher that season, so I was there mainly to encourage him.

Glen Earl Robinson was on the team but certainly wasn't one of the star players. For one thing he was just ten years old. For another he was short, fat, and slow, and couldn't hit very well and rarely caught a fly ball, even in practice.

But you never saw anyone prouder to put on a Cardinals uniform than Glen Earl. Usually he sat on the bench until late in the game when he might go in to play right field for an inning if we were far enough ahead.

This particular night, however, we were down to nine players, so Glen Earl started in right field against the Braves. Sure enough, with two out and two runners on base in the first inning, the batter drove a fly ball to right field. It almost hit Glen Earl in the glove. Almost. Instead, it rolled all the way to the fence, while he ran after it. The Braves scored two runs and would have had a third except the runner slipped down rounding third base.

"That's all right, Glen Earl," I said to him when he came in after the third out. Glen Earl was practically in tears.

By the sixth and last inning, the Braves had scored just one more run, and the Cardinals had scored three, so we were tied 3-3, with two outs and nobody on base. Glen Earl came to bat. He had struck out his first time up and popped out his second time.

This time he hit a slow roller down the third base line. Glen Earl started chugging toward first base, running as hard as he could but not getting there very fast. The third baseman bobbled the ball but still would have had time to throw Glen Earl out at first. But the throw sailed over the first baseman's head.

Glen Earl finally got to first base and headed for second, even though the first base coach was hollering, "No, Glen Earl, stop, come back to first!"

The first baseman retrieved the errant throw and still had plenty of time to throw Glen Earl out at second. He made a perfect throw to second base. Glen Earl was only about halfway there, so he turned around and started chugging back to first. Instead of running him down, the second baseman threw the ball to the first baseman. Once again it sailed over his head.

Glen Earl turned around and ran to second base. But he didn't stop there. He headed for third. The first baseman chased down the ball and threw it to the third baseman, but it bounced in front of him and rolled to the fence, way down the left field line.

Glen Earl touched third base and started running for home. By now everyone was out of the dugout jumping and cheering and waving him on. The left fielder came up and picked up the ball, but by then Glen Earl was halfway to home base. The throw was wide to the right and Glen Earl slid home with the winning run. Cardinals 4, Braves 3.

That night was when I gave Glen Earl his nickname, "Flash." And he's been Flash ever since. In high school Flash was a pretty fair offensive guard on the Bandits football team. He never did gain much speed, but he worked hard and he never lacked for confidence. He's still short and squatty today, but he has been a high school football coach for a good many years over in Anderson.

"Hey, Mac," Flash said, "you remember when I hit that inside the park home run?"

"Flash," I said, "it was your blinding speed that made it possible."

Flash flashed that big grin of his. "It was, wasn't it?"

31

Mister Morgan's Model A

Coleman Springs has had only two postmasters in the last eighty-eight years. I have served for the past thirty-five years, but I still have a ways to go before I catch up with Mister Morgan, who was postmaster for fifty-three years.

Everyone called Mister Morgan "Mister Morgan," even his wife, Helene. His first name was Frank, and surely he was called that as a young man, and maybe Helene called him Frank in private. But by the time I knew him he was Mister Morgan.

I've never known a more dignified and proper man. He always wore a suit to work and always a bow tie. I don't think he even owned a four-in-hand tie. He wore a bow tie, and of course he tied it himself. No clip-ons for him. He would be mortified.

He addressed everyone as Mister or Miss or Mrs., never by their first name, even the little children. He called me Mister Spearman from the time I first toddled into the post

office until the day he died, three years after he finally retired and turned over the keys to me as the new postmaster.

Mister Morgan kept a pocket watch in the vest pocket of his suit. He had been given the watch as his high school graduation present, and it was one of his most prized possessions.

His *most* prized possession, however, was the Model A Ford he drove to work every day. Mister Morgan and Helene lived just three blocks from the post office, and he easily could have walked to work, and in fact did in his younger days—before the Model A.

He drove an early Model T back then, and you had to turn a crank to get it started, and sometime Mister Morgan would just give up and walk rather than get his suit all sweaty from the effort.

When the Model A came out in 1927, he was the first person in town to buy one. It was a two-tone sedan and quite stylish. Every morning he would drive it to work and park it right in front of the post office where he could keep an eye on it. He drove it until he lapsed into a coma, three weeks before he died.

Well, not that particular Model A. He was on his second one by then, or rather his third one, depending on how you look at it. He liked the first one so much, he figured there would never be a better car ever produced, so he bought another Model A in 1929 and hung it from the rafter of his garage. The next year he bought a third one. Hung it in the garage as well.

He drove the first Model A for more than twenty-five years before finally retiring it to the garage. He left the second one—a red model—hanging and brought out the

1930 model, which was tan. At his age, he figured, a tan car seemed more proper than a red car. He drove that tan Model A until his death.

Folks had pretty much forgotten about the red one still hanging in the garage. After all, it had been more than forty years since he bought it. Helene was about the only person who remembered it was still there.

Helene herself never learned to drive, never thought she needed to. Mister Morgan would take her to the store and to church or she would ride with one of her friends to study club or garden club.

"Mac," she told me after the funeral, "Mister Morgan would want you to have those cars."

I was a young family man then and I drove a station wagon, which we needed with our two children and their various friends and pets. I usually walked to work anyway, or Mary would drive me, and we didn't have a large enough garage for a second car, much less three more. And, I have to admit, at the time I thought driving a Model A would make me seem old, like Mister Morgan.

I thanked Helene for the offer but told her I just didn't have anywhere to keep the cars. She offered to let me keep them in her garage as long as she was alive, but I didn't think she would be around very long herself. She was in her eighties, and sure enough within a year she had moved to a nursing home in Georgia so she could be close to a niece she was fond of. Helene and Mister Morgan didn't have any children.

Anyway, I told Helene I would help her find someone who would appreciate the cars and would take good care of them.

The Ford dealer—we had a Ford and a Chevy dealership back then—was John Tellis. His father, Edward Tellis, had sold the Model A's to Mister Morgan. I told John about the cars. He didn't even know about the one still hanging in the garage, but of course he had admired the 1930 Model A that Mister Morgan drove around town and he remembered the 1927 car, now retired.

He was thrilled with the idea of owning the cars and promised he would contact Helene and make her a fair offer for them, which he did.

John kept the cars in great running order, even restoring the 1927 Model A to where it ran and looked like a brand new car. Eventually he moved the dealership closer to Granger Falls, but he kept the old Ford building here where he stores his cars. He and his son Jeb have added eight more Model A's to those first three, plus several other old cars and trucks, and during the Ice Cream Festival and Homecoming they get friends to drive them in the parade and then they park the cars around the square for the day.

Back when he was in high school, Jeb did a term paper on "Mister Morgan and His Model A's," and in the front window of the 1927 car he has placed a sign telling about Mister Morgan and showing a photograph of him in suit and bow tie standing beside the car.

Even though Mister Morgan has been dead nearly thirty-five years, his legacy lives on.

Oh, Helene also offered me Mister Morgan's other prized possession, the pocket watch. I carry it to this day.

32

Father Dominic

St. John's Catholic Church in Coleman Springs is quite small, but every Sunday morning at eight o'clock Father Dominic serves communion to the two dozen or so faithful parishioners. Then he drives over to the much larger St. Mary's at Walnut Cove and conducts the eleven o'clock service there.

Father Dominic has been the priest at both parishes for thirty years or so. Everyone in town knows and loves Father Dominic. When anyone from Coleman Springs is in the hospital in the city, whether they're Catholic or not, they get a visit and a prayer from Father Dominic. Every Tuesday morning, he goes to breakfast with the pastors of the other churches in Coleman Springs, and several of them have turned to him for counsel when they were facing a crisis.

We've never had very many Catholics in Coleman Springs, and for years they had to go over to St. Mary's or one of the Granger Falls churches to worship. Father Dominic

helped the small group organize and build St. John's, and he has been their priest ever since.

Father Dominic has to be in his late eighties and he's been a priest for fifty-five years. The *Granger Falls Gazette* ran a nice article about him a few months ago on his fifty-fifth anniversary in the priesthood.

A lot of folks didn't know the whole story about Father Dominic until that article came out. He doesn't talk about it often.

As a very young man, he was stationed in the Pacific during World War II and he saw some of the worst action. Most of the young soldiers in his platoon were killed or wounded.

He wasn't Father Dominic then. He was Bob Smith from Montana, and he wasn't Catholic. In fact, he had never even met a Catholic, as far as he could remember, until the war.

A Catholic chaplain served with Bob's platoon, and the young men came to love and respect the priest for the fearless way in which he ministered to the wounded and dying. He was right there with them during the heaviest action, administering last rites to the fatally wounded, helping those with lesser wounds get medical attention, comforting and encouraging the soldiers—boys who suddenly had to become men—and helping them deal with their fears. He often wrote letters to the families of the soldiers who were killed in action, telling them what fine young men their sons and brothers were.

One night the platoon came under fierce attack. One of the soldiers was hit in the chest and legs. He wasn't killed but couldn't move. The priest rushed to him and fell on top of him while the firing continued. A bullet pierced the priest's neck and he died instantly, still lying on top of the wounded soldier.

After the battle, the soldier was evacuated and eventually recovered. That soldier was Bob Smith.

Bob Smith returned home, enrolled in a Catholic college, and committed his life to being a priest. He felt he should take up the cause of the man who had given his own life to save Bob's life.

That chaplain, that Catholic priest in the Pacific, went by the name of Father Dominic.

Inscribed in stone just inside the front door of St. John's Catholic Church is a quotation from the book of St. John, chapter fifteen, verse thirteen: "Greater love hath no man than this: that he lay down his life for his friends."

33

Golfing in Coleman Springs

You know Ed Magnusson, the former pro football player who now hosts the TV show "Par for the Course"? Ed goes around the country playing golf at scenic and out-of-the-way places and doing pieces about them for the show. He has played some of the greatest, and oddest, golf courses in the country.

Well, we're all kind of buzzing about him and his crew coming to play at the Coleman Springs Municipal Golf Course. We're going to be on national TV!

A few months ago our mayor, Admiral Drexel Bryant, wrote Ed and invited him to come to Coleman Springs. The mayor noted that our golf course has six distinguishing features:

1. It only has eight holes instead of nine.
2. There is a water hazard on every hole.

3. The third hole is a par 7.
4. Par for the entire course is 31.
5. No one has ever shot par.
6. There is a landing strip for private planes right by the clubhouse.

Ed wanted to know more, so he called the mayor.

"Why only eight holes?" Ed asked.

"Ed, you're not going to believe me when I tell you," Drexel said. "The reason we have just eight holes is because the sixth hole washed away in a flood about twenty years ago.

"I told you there is a water hazard on every hole. Well, it wasn't designed that way. We had a little creek and a small lake, but when they built a big recreational lake north of town it overflowed into the creek, which in turn overflowed into the golf course lake.

"One year there was so much overflow that the whole course was flooded, and by the time everything was sorted out, we had lost the sixth hole altogether and had creeks or lake fingers on all the other holes."

"So tell me about that par 7," Ed said.

"Well, when we lost the sixth hole, we had to dogleg the fifth hole around the lake, and it turned out to be a very long hole, about 750 yards with three water hazards. It's a tough hole, Ed."

"And yet," Ed asked, "par for the entire course is just 31?"

"Yes, I know it's strange," the mayor said, "but when the course was reconfigured, we ended up with two very short par 3s to go with the three original par 3s. So we have five par 3s, one par 4, one par 5, and one par 7. Total par is 31."

"But no one has ever shot par?" Ed asked.

"No," Drexel said. "It's the water hazards, Ed. They're pretty tough to avoid."

"What's the lowest anyone has shot?" Ed asked.

"About three years ago in conjunction with our ice cream festival," the mayor said, "we sponsored a golf exhibition featuring a couple of pros from the senior tour and two local guys who had won the course championship. It was quite a show, but one of our local guys ended up winning it with a thirty-two, one over par. That's the best anyone's ever done. By the way, the pros shot thirty-five and thirty-seven."

"Tell me about the landing strip. Is there a water hazard on it as well?" Ed chuckled.

"No, it's high and dry. It also serves as our little local airport, but planes can taxi over to the clubhouse if they want to. It can handle small jets, and we get celebrities flying in here from time to time, mainly to play the par 7 hole."

"Do you play golf, mayor?" Ed asked.

"Yes, but not very well," Drexel said, "especially not on this course!"

"Well, you've sold me," Ed said. "This is a course I've got to see."

"Do you want me to line up some local players to play with you?"

"I always like to have a threesome, as you know if you've seen the show—a local player, a pro, and myself," Ed said. "I will come a couple of days early so I can play the course two or three times and not completely embarrass myself when I play on camera. I'll pick the pro. Why don't you get five or six of your best players there in Coleman Springs to play with me during the practice rounds and then I can select one who I think would work best on camera?"

They agreed on a date in about three weeks. Meanwhile, Drexel faces a serious political problem. As soon as word got out, he had calls from about twenty golfers wanting to play with Ed. He has to choose no more than six.

"It's simple, Drexel," I told him. "Just take bribes."

"Thanks for your help, Mac," he said.

34

The Best Burger in Town

I think I told you that churches outnumber saloons in Coleman Springs by five to two, and nearly everyone in town thinks that's a good thing.

There was a time in our history, many years ago, when it was the other way around, or even worse. We had a lot more bars than churches. But that was back before we became civilized, before we had women and children and indoor plumbing.

Now we have just two saloons—Pete's Bar & Grill and You Have the Wrong Number.

You Have the Wrong Number is run by Jacqui Everett, who was known as Jacqui Smythe when she was a, well, she was a hooker in Denver. She kind of cleaned up her act, married Teller Everett, bought a double-wide on the outskirts of Coleman Springs, and opened Jacqui's Joint.

It didn't take her long to figure out that when women called looking for their husbands or boyfriends, they didn't

want to find them at Jacqui's Joint. So she changed the name of the place. Now when she answers the phone, she can say with integrity and impunity "You Have the Wrong Number."

Seems to have worked.

Meanwhile, Pete Peterson doesn't try to disguise his place. It's Pete's Bar & Grill. Simple. Straightforward. Nothing deceptive. Well, not if you don't count the missing "e".

Pete Peterson, like most Pete Petersons I suspect, hasn't always been Pete. In fact, his mother had higher hopes for him when he was born. She named him Aristotle Peterson, thinking that maybe if the Aristotle didn't take, perhaps he would be called Aris.

And he was. Until sixth grade. Aris was the second-biggest kid in sixth grade. The biggest kid, Roman Jackson, didn't like the name Aris. He started calling him Pete.

Pete didn't consider it an affront to his manhood or anything, so he began answering to Pete, and has ever since, even after Roman Jackson was sent off to reform school.

Pete had several careers, even repeated a few of them, before settling down and opening his own saloon a decade or so ago. He had his name put up in lights, Pete's Bar & Grill.

Only problem was, less than six months after he opened, the last "e" in Pete burned out, and at the time he didn't have the money to fix it. So his place became "Pet 's Bar & Grill." And that's what it has been ever since.

Doesn't matter. We all know there are two saloons in Coleman Springs. Pete's, or Pet 's, is the only one that someone like me would frequent. I wouldn't be caught in Jacqui's Joint, or You Have the Wrong Number, or whatever she decides to call it.

Actually, I wouldn't go to Pet's if it was just a bar. It's the second half of the name—& Grill—that draws me in. Mary, too. She doesn't mind going to Pet's. In fact, we both look forward to it.

You should know that under the neon sign for "Pet's Bar & Grill" is a printed sign that proclaims "Biggest and Best Buffalo Burgers."

Pete isn't bragging. It's the truth, as far as I know. Now, I can't claim to have eaten that many buffalo burgers in my life, but if there is a bigger or better one than Pet's, you will have to prove it to me.

Pete's Buffalo Burger is not a third of a pound or a half a pound of meat. It's two-thirds of a pound, served on an *eight-inch* homemade bun with a side order of what he calls Buffalo Chips.

Pete doesn't have a menu. You have two choices: Buffalo Burger Basket, or Buffalo Burger Basket with Cheese. They cost the same.

Mary and I always split a Buffalo Burger Basket with Cheese. Pete cuts the burger into two almost equal slices, giving me maybe a slightly larger piece. We nearly always have to ask for a piece of foil so we can wrap up the leftovers and take them home.

And good? Let me tell you, it's the best burger—beef, bison, or otherwise—I have ever put in my mouth.

That's why Mary and I don't feel like we're sneaking out to go to Pet's. Plenty of other "respectable"—that is to say Presbyterian—folks go there as well.

We sit in the front room, of course. The Coleman Springs "no smoking" ordinance doesn't apply to saloons, but Pete made the front room "no smoking" a few years ago, while accommodating the smokers in the back room.

Pet 's gets a bit crowded, especially since the *Granger Falls Gazette* named it the Best Burger in the area. It's worse on the weekends, so we tend to go on Monday or Tuesday nights. Maybe we'll see you there.

35

Bicycle Bandits

The Bicycle Bandits have hit our town.

There must be eighty or a hundred of them or more, all wearing bandanas pulled up to cover their faces like old-time train robbers, all riding bicycles. I saw them riding through downtown a little while ago.

The Bicycle Bandits are led by Vern and Verna Kester and their high school daughter, LaVerna, and eighth grade son, Vernon. Riding behind them are kids of various ages as well as their parents and, in some cases, grandparents.

They plan to "hold up" every house in town before the day is over. My wife Mary said they've already been to our house. She handed over what they demanded.

What they demanded was food. Canned food.

The Bicycle Bandits are collecting food for the Mission Action Project. The Kesters came up with the idea and enlisted other members of The Church of the Living Word. They talked it up with their friends and neighbors. Next

thing you knew, the Bicycle Bandits were a force to be reckoned with.

They decided to "terrorize" the town on Thursday afternoon after school. It was an early-release day, with the children getting out at noon. They went home and got their bikes and bandanas and toy guns and gathered at The Church of the Living Word, on the outskirts of town, which is to say about half a mile from the center of town.

By 2:30 they began knocking on doors and ringing doorbells and sticking their toy guns in the faces of startled residents.

Pretty soon nearly everyone in town was laughing about the Bicycle Bandits and telling how they had retreated to their pantries, at gunpoint, and retrieved cans of corn, beans, peas, and okra.

Betsy Kennedy said she thought she was finally going to get rid of that can of beets she had had in her pantry since Lord knows when.

But the masked Bandit waved his toy pistol at her and said, "No beets."

Then he corrected himself, "I mean, no beets, ma'am."

When Rhoda Vazquez opened the door and saw the little masked Bandits, they thought she was screaming. But she was just talking in her normal voice, "IS THIS A HOLD-UP? PLEASE DON'T TAKE MY WEDDING RING."

The Bandits assured her that they didn't want her wedding ring.

"You can't eat a wedding ring, ma'am," one of them said. "We want food! Canned goods."

"HOW ABOUT A CAN OF APPLESAUCE!" she asked. "WILL THAT BE ALL RIGHT?"

A little Bandit waved his gun, "Two cans would be even better!"

Rhoda handed over two cans of applesauce and ran to call Galindo and tell him they had been "ROBBED!"

Claire Fletcher told the Bandits at her door that all she had was some "Presbyterian peas." Would that be all right?

"Yes, please," a Bandit replied.

Tonya Davis got home from work to find masked Bandits waiting for her in the driveway. She had stopped by the supermarket in Granger Falls on the way home to pick up a few things. By the time she got in her house, she had even fewer.

Ida Frazier "donated" three cans of carrots she had. "I hope they don't make anyone sick," she told her friend Marge Blanchard. "I can't remember when I bought them."

Pop Ellison seemed confused at first when he answered the door and saw three little masked Bandits. But it didn't take him long to figure out what was going on. He gave them two cans of fruit cocktail. They thanked him. He thanked *them*. "My daughter serves me fruit cocktail every night."

Janelle Perry came out with a can of sliced pineapple and a jar of crunchy peanut butter. Annetta Coleman unloaded three big cans of asparagus she had bought for a dinner party but decided not to use, and a can of black olives.

The Bandits were afraid to go to Zolly Quivnik's door. He's too strange, they thought. But finally one of them volunteered. Zolly nodded, without saying anything, and returned with four cans of evaporated milk.

Daniel Boone came home from the store, fixed himself a bite of lunch, and was about ready to go to bed when the doorbell rang. The Bandit relieved him of a box of rice and a can of green chiles.

When Erick Dawkins opened the door, the Bandits caught the whiff of an aromatic candle burning in the front room. Erick gave them two bars of soap and a plastic bottle of shampoo. Not exactly edible, but oh well.

Wendy Day wasn't predicting the weather that day. She forked over a can of snow peas. Ida Mae Gentry gave her Bandits a can of macadamia nuts she had brought home from Hawaii.

Lacy Curry was all smiles. "Oh, you little darlings," she said to the four Bandits at her door. She returned with an armful of canned vegetables and fruit.

The mayor, Admiral Bryant was home when the Bandits pounded on his door. You can probably guess what he came up with.

Two cans of navy beans.

And so it went, all afternoon. It was the most successful food drive in the history of Coleman Springs.

36

Bigboy vs. Tiny

Bigboy Leonard is forty-two years old. His cousin, Tiny Massingale, is forty-one. They have been friends, as well as cousins, all their lives. But they've always been intensely competitive.

Bigboy is, as you might expect from his name, quite large. And Tiny is anything but tiny. They were always the biggest kids in junior high and high school, and today they are still the largest men in town—and that's saying something.

They're also the strongest men in town, without question. Which one is stronger? Well, that's been the continuing debate ever since they were children.

In high school, Bigboy was the district shot put champion his sophomore year and Tiny, a freshman, was second. The next year Tiny won, beating Bigboy by three and a half inches. Bigboy reclaimed the title the next year by a mere one inch. By the time Tiny was a senior, Bigboy had graduated, so Tiny won district that year by seventeen feet.

They both played on the offensive line for the Coleman Springs Bandits, and what a fearsome twosome they made. Both tipped the scales at more than three hundred pounds, even then. And they've not gone on any crash diets since.

Their arms are bigger than most men's legs. Their necks—well, they really don't have necks. Their muscles bulge all over. They are not rolling in fat, except maybe a little that hangs over their belts.

Bigboy is taller by three inches. Tiny is a little bigger in the shoulders and legs. When they walk into a room together, people can't help but stare. Together they weigh around seven hundred pounds.

A few weeks ago Preston Day, who is president of the Lions Club this year, came up with a great idea for a fund-raiser.

"Let's have a heavyweight arm-wrestling match between Bigboy and Tiny," he proposed. The club members thought it was a super idea and they approached the cousins about it.

"I'll smash him like a bug," Bigboy bellowed.

"I'll crush him like an aluminum can," Tiny countered.

HEAVYWEIGHT ARM-WRESTLING

Bigboy Leonard, 365 pounds
vs.
Tiny Massingale, 355 pounds

Coleman Springs High School Gym
Admission $3

Benefiting the Coleman Springs Lions Club

The match was set for the high school gym. A table would be set up in the middle of the room. Best two out of three.

Posters were printed up and displayed around town and even in Granger Falls.

They sold seats only on the "home" side of the gym so everyone would be close to the action. More than three hundred people bought tickets.

Mary and I couldn't pass it up. We got there early and had seats on the third row right next to Bobo—I mean Bo—and Betsy Kennedy and in front of Pete Harwood and Morris Jenkins, who are on speaking terms again.

Preston Day hammed it up, imitating the announcer at a world championship heavyweight boxing match. "Ladies and gentlemen, welcome to Championship Arm Wrestling right here in Coleman Springs. Tonight's event will be a best two out of three.

"In the red shorts, wearing a white t-shirt and black shoes, standing six feet, two inches, and weighing 365 pounds, Mister BIGGGGBOYYYYY Leonard."

Stomps, whoops, cheers.

"In the black shorts, wearing a gray t-shirt and white shoes, standing five feet, eleven inches, and weighing 355 pounds, Mister TIIIIINEEEEY Massingale."

More stomps, whoops, cheers.

The referee, the singing barber Pierce Brock (and third largest man in town), explained the rules and had them shake hands. Then the cousins took their seats across the four-by-six oak table from each other. Dr. Taylor Campbell sat nearby, just in case.

Bigboy and Tiny clasped each other's right hand and leaned in on their right elbows, which would always have to be touching the table. Their left hands gripped their own left knees.

Pierce gave the signal and the contest began. Bigboy tried for a quick takedown, but Tiny was up to the challenge and held him in check. Both men grunted loudly as they tried to push their opponent's arm toward the table.

They groaned. They roared. They turned red in the face. But neither one budged.

The crowd hollered encouragement. "Come on, Bigboy!" "Take him down, Tiny!"

Their muscles bulged. Their stomachs tightened. Their backs and legs strained. But neither one budged.

After ten minutes, neither cousin had been able to move the other's arm more than an inch or two. Both seemed at the point of exhaustion, but neither one would give in. Another five minutes went by. No movement either direction.

Tiny tried taking the offense and moved Bigboy's arm maybe two inches, but Bigboy held on and gradually moved Tiny's arm back an inch. Tiny roared and gave it all he had and moved Bigboy's arm an inch or so. Bigboy roared back and leaned in closer, putting more weight on his right elbow, and moved Tiny's arm back to the original center position.

Tiny leaned in harder on his right elbow and let out another loud grunt. Bigboy matched him grunt for grunt, muscle for muscle. Both men were leaning in hard, so close that their heads were almost touching.

Then, suddenly, there was a break.

Bigboy didn't break.

Tiny didn't break.

The table broke. The rustic oak table all of a sudden couldn't take it anymore. The legs just snapped and the table crashed to the floor.

The cousins collapsed on top of the busted table and on top of each other. The crowd gasped as the cousins and the table lay in a pile on the floor. Dr. Taylor Campbell ran over to see if the men were hurt.

Tiny, who was on top, slowly got to his feet. Then he took Bigboy's right hand and pulled him to his feet. The crowd came to their feet cheering. Bigboy and Tiny held each other's arm up high in a victory salute. The crowd roared its approval.

"Ladies and gentlemen," announced Preston Day, "we will not declare tonight's decision a draw. Instead, we will declare it a victory for Bigboy Leonard and Tiny Massingale. The loser, as you can see, is the oak table from my study. Thank you, Bigboy and Tiny, and thank you all for coming out for this historic event. Good night."

Counting the tickets sold and concession sales, the Lions Club made well over a thousand dollars. Bigboy and Tiny each received a trophy and a gift certificate to the Coleman Springs Steak House. Preston Day had to go out and buy a new conference table.

So which cousin is stronger? We may never know.

37

Festival Time

Like a lot of Coleman Springs families, Mary and I have a full house this weekend for the tenth annual Coleman Springs Ice Cream Festival.

Daughter Esther and her husband Russ Fairly arrived on Thursday with their two daughters, Cara and Jenn. Son Bryant and his wife Hailey got here Friday afternoon, but Bryant Jr. won't be able to come this year. He's working this summer in Alaska, earning money for college.

Russ and Esther and the girls were anxious to eat Mary's cooking, so Thursday night she fixed smothered steak and four or five vegetables and her yeast rolls, and we stuffed ourselves so much we almost didn't have room for apple pie. Almost.

Friday night, after Bryant and Hailey joined us, was fried chicken night. The eight of us devoured three chickens, leaving little behind but the bones. We topped off that meal with chocolate cake. But no ice cream. Tradition is that no one in Coleman Springs serves ice cream on Friday during festival week. We make everyone wait one more day.

The festival begins early Saturday morning with the half-mile backwards walk. The Timms sisters got the idea for the backwards walk from watching teen-age boys wearing their caps backwards. All participants are given a cap, which they must wear backwards for the full half-mile. Since they are walking backwards, their caps are actually moving forward. You just have to be there.

Next is the parade which starts at the high school, moves three blocks down Main Street, goes around the square, and back to the high school on Orchard Street. Since it's summer, we don't get any high school or college marching bands, so the sisters organized the Coleman Springs Kazoo Band to march and play and lead the parade.

They are followed by the Coleman Springs Cheerleaders, throwing tiny footballs to the crowd with the Coleman Springs Bandits football schedule printed on them.

The parade marshal this year is Father Dominic, riding in a white convertible.

Several other convertibles follow, including one proudly driven by Galindo Vazquez with his new wife, Rhoda, sitting in the back, smiling and waving to the crowd.

Marshal Dillon is dressed up like the TV marshal and shooting off his cap pistol in the back of a yellow convertible. A new couple in town, the Fosters, are riding in the back of a convertible with signs advertising our "Come Home to Coleman Springs" campaign.

The Coleman Springs Family Council has a group of children riding on a flatbed and singing "It's a Small World After All," over and over and over. On another flatbed are The Canes, a walking stick drill team from the Senior Citizens Center.

The Bicycle Bandits are decked out in cowboy hats, Bicycle Bandits t-shirts, and jeans, with bandanas covering their faces. Bigboy Leonard and Tiny Massingale are in the back of two pickups side by side, with a table stretched between the trucks, and they are hamming it up, pretending to be arm wrestling.

John and Jeb Tellis and their classic car club usually bring up the rear of the parade with their Model A's and other old cars. But this year falling in line behind the cars are the motorcyclists from the BBA Bike Club. "We're baaaaaaack!" they yell to the crowd.

After the parade, everyone gathers in the park behind the post office for the official opening of the main event: eating ice cream.

First, Dr. C. J. Fletcher, being the newest minister in town, is asked to pray. It is, of course, short: "Thank you, God, for ice cream. Amen."

Patti Timms Oliver serves Mayor Bryant a scoop of her strawberry ice cream, and the mayor pronounces it fit for consumption and announces, "Let the festival begin!"

The rest of the day is a time for sampling ice cream and visiting old friends who have come back to town.

Churches and other organizations set up tables and booths under the shade of trees around the square, and people go from booth to booth to taste the various flavors, at one dollar a scoop. This year there are a record number of booths—forty-three. It used to be, when the festival started with sixteen tables, that some men would try to sample every flavor. But not even Bigboy and Tiny could begin to eat forty-three scoops.

St. John's Catholic Church features Nancy Timms' sister, Bettylee Morgan, and her rum ice cream, which always seems to be especially popular with the Baptists. It's the only ice cream booth at the festival, probably in the whole country, that requires an ID card showing proof of age. The Mothers Against Drunk Driving stand by to offer anyone a ride home who has consumed too much rum ice cream. Some prefer to find a spot on the grass and just sleep it off.

The forty-three booths, on average, will serve between two and three hundred scoops of ice cream each, or roughly ten to twelve thousand scoops altogether. Our little town of eight hundred swells to three or four times that size on festival day.

By mid-afternoon people have had their fill of ice cream and begin to drift off to the comfort of their homes for a nap, and the festival is over. Visitors take time to look at the classic cars parked around the square, do a little shopping at Coleman Springs Hardware, maybe get a haircut from the singing barber, or buy a festival t-shirt or a Walking Backwards cap.

Possibly they dream a little about what it would be like to live in what appears to them a small, peaceful, ideal village, away from the demands of the city.

Of course, we know that we are not untouched by the tides and tempests that affect us all. But on festival day, like pretty much every day in Coleman Springs, we are reminded to be grateful that we live in a place endowed with a sweet taste for living and a generous scoop of good will.

Appendix 1

Some of the people who live in Coleman Springs

Baker, Rev. Andrew—pastor of First Baptist Church
Boone, Daniel—co-owner of a convenience store
Brock, Pierce—singing barber
Bryant, Drexel—mayor, former presidential advisor
Bryant, Miriam—first lady of Coleman Springs
Campbell, Taylor—town doctor
Coleman, Annabelle—fifth grader
Coleman, Evan—owner of Coleman Springs Steak House, father of
    Annabelle
Curry, Lacy—writer of postcards to presidents
Dawkins, Broder and Erick—brothers
Day, Wendy and Preston—she's a TV weather forecaster, he is presi-
    dent of the Lions Club
Dillon, Marshal—co-owner of a convenience store
Ellison, Diane—daughter of Pop
Ellison, Pop—retired accountant, colorful walking attire
Father Dominic—Catholic priest, war veteran
Fletcher, C. J.—short-winded Presbyterian preacher
Fletcher, Claire—preacher's wife
Forrester, Miss Effie—retired third grade teacher
Frazier, Ida—elderly resident

Gentry, Ida Mae and Howard—strict grammarian and her husband
Gibbons, George—poet laureate
Happenhouser, Louise—world traveler, sister of Ida Mae
Harwood, Pete—bank president
Jenkins, Morris—hardware store owner
Johnson, Possum—handyman
Kennedy, Bo and Betsy—Bo is a war hero
Kester family—Vern, Verna, LaVerna, Vernon; leaders of Bicycle
    Bandits
Landers, Opal—bad driver
Leonard, Bigboy—largest man in town
Massingale, Tiny—second largest man in town
Matson, Banjo—banjo player and town character
Maybridge, Lester—plumber
McDermand, Kevan and Paige—parents of Rainey
McDermand, Rainey—most beautiful in every way
Pearson, Bambi—owns Comb Aplomb beauty shop, avid reader
Pernfors, Emily—co-founder of literacy council
Perry, Janelle—literacy council founder
Peterson, Aristotle (Pete)—owner of Pete's Bar & Grill, best burger
    in town
Phillips, Jacob—homebuilder and husband of Cindi Timms
Pratt, Jameson—high school math teacher
Pritchert, Simon—genius farmer and speller
Quivnik, Zolly—recluse
Sanders, Elliott—pastor of The Church of the Living Word
Simpson, Miss Jenny—librarian
Spearman, Mac—postmaster, narrator
Spearman, Mary—Mac's wife, great cook
Steckham, Marti and Mandi—twin fifth graders
Tellis, John and Jeb—Ford dealers
Timms, Rollie and Nancy—parents of Timms sisters
Timms sisters
    Ashli—nurse
    Cindi (Phillips)—former mayor
    Patti (Oliver)—oldest of the sisters
    Tammi—second oldest sister
Vazquez, Galindo and Rhoda—newlyweds

Appendix 2

Coleman Springs businesses, churches, and organizations

Businesses

Bales Grocery & Drug
Campbell Medical Clinic
Coleman Springs Barber Shop
Coleman Springs Hardware
Coleman Springs Insurance
Coleman Springs Realty
Coleman Springs State & National Bank
Coleman Springs Steak House
Comb Aplomb Beauty Salon
Daniel Boone & Marshal Dillon Express
Hair With Flair Beauty Shop
Highway Gas & Go
House of Hope Day Care Center
Lester's Plumbing
Oliver Law Office
People's Dollar Place

Pete's Bar & Grill
Pizza Palace
Segada Auto Sales & Service
Waverly's Feed & Seed
You Have the Wrong Number (bar)

Churches:

Coleman Springs United Methodist Church
First Baptist Church
Pioneer Presbyterian Church
St. John's Catholic Church
The Church of the Living Word

Organizations:

Bicycle Bandits
Coleman Springs Book Club
Coleman Springs Chamber of Commerce
Coleman Springs Garden Club
Coleman Springs Ice Cream Festival
Coleman Springs Lions Club
Coleman Springs Literacy Council
Coleman Springs Municipal Golf Course
Coleman Springs PTA
Coleman Springs Public Library
Coleman Springs Senior Citizens Center
Come Home to Coleman Springs
Democrats of Coleman Springs
Friends of the Library
Methodist Men's Fellowship
Mission Action Project
Mothers Against Drunk Driving
Red Cross, Coleman Springs Chapter
Republican Party of Coleman Springs
Women's Bible Study